Puerto Vallarta Squeeze

*Also by Robert James Waller
in Thorndike Large Print* ®

The Bridges of Madison County
Slow Waltz in Cedar Bend
Old Songs in a New Café
Border Music

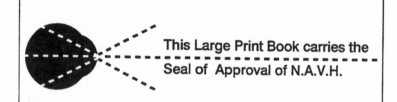

Puerto Vallarta Squeeze

(The Run for *el Norte*)

Robert James Waller

Thorndike Press • Thorndike, Maine

Published in 1996 by arrangement with Warner Books Inc.

Thorndike Large Print ® Basic Series.

The tree indicium is a trademark of Thorndike Press.

The text of this Large Print edition is unabridged.
Other aspects of the book may vary from the original edition.

Set in 16 pt. News Plantin.

Printed in the United States on permanent paper.

Library of Congress Cataloging in Publication Data

Waller, Robert James, 1939–
    Puerto Vallarta squeeze / Robert James Waller.
      p.   cm.
  ISBN 0-7862-0558-X (lg. print : hc)
  ISBN 0-7862-0559-8 (lg. print : lsc)
    1. Large type books. I. Title.
  [PS3573.A4347P84 1996]
  813'.54—dc20

                                             95-33517

For flowers
        and sad songs.

And for Jim Flansburg and Jim Gannon
who trusted in me, early on.

I mean, Luz was really good, kind in her heart and all that. Christ, she was just a simple country girl, doing the best she could for herself. You should've seen her — she was knock-'em-dead beautiful sometimes, most of the time, with a flower in her hair and pink lipstick on. Even in that cheap straw hat Clayton Price bought her. I still see her that way . . . in that cheap straw hat and yellow dress and him carrying her across a little river in the Mexican backcountry — a butterfly in the keep of a fer-de-lance. . . . Clayton Price, that sonuvabitch. Still, you had to admire him in a perverse way. I even felt sorry for him a couple of times.

Danny Eugene Pastor, October 1994

Clayton Price's edge was that he never hesitated, never once, not as long as I knew him. While the rest of the world was standin' around waitin' for the bell to ring, he was already out of his corner and swingin'. In the old days, he'd have been gone while the bad guys were still gassin' their trucks. Can't figure out what happened, what he musta been thinkin' there at the end.

MacKenzie Watt, mercenary

Wherever it is Men Go

This guy Lobo, whose real and true name was Wolfgang Fink, played better than good flamenco guitar in a place called Mamma Mia in Puerto Vallarta. Had a partner name of Willie Royal, tall gangly guy who was balding a little early and wore glasses and played hot gypsy-jazz violin. They'd worked out a repertoire of their own tunes, "Improvisation #18" and "Gypsy Rook" as examples, played 'em high and hard, rolled through "Amsterdam" and "The Sultan's Dream" with enough power to set you two times free or even beyond that when the day had been tolerable and the night held promise. Lobo, sun worn and hard lined in the face, looking over at Willie Royal bobbing and weaving and twisting his face into a mean imitation of a death mask when he really got into it, right wrist looking almost limp but moving his bow at warp speed across the strings, punctuated here and there by Lobo's stabbing ruscados and finger tapping on the guitar top.

Good music, wonderful music, tight and

wild all at the same time. On those nights when the sweat ran down your back and veneered your face and the gringitas looked good enough to swallow whole — knowing too they looked just that way and them watching the crowd to see who might be man enough to try it — people would be riding on the music, drinking and clapping in flamenco time, dancing around the dinner tables.

It was crazy back then, crazy good if you didn't look too close. The music as a mustering-out call at first, then later in the evening as wallpaper for the nighttime thrusts of a rumpled expatriate army whose soldiers never spoke of bolixed lives and stained little souls. Upriver Sally was working in bronze and Hillside Dave was foundering in what he called his "Regressive Matisse" period. Most of the rest were just talking about doing something — nothing small, understand — the "gonnas" per hour roughly equaling the number of tequilas consumed. From any kind of distance at all, it looked like amoebas navigating a glass slide, on the search for the nearest pile of food and being more or less content with what they found, mostly less. Less seemed easier and didn't require a reduction in beach time.

But none of that mattered unless you

thought about it. And thought was to be restrained, if not suppressed, regarded as some antiquity from a former world. A world from which all had fled . . . or had been released, depending on your charity and point of view. Reflection or remembrance, any or all of that, pulled up things best left buried deep and covered over. Sifted through, boiled down, flipped twice and double fried, it had become a simple place to be. A kind of perverted Darwinism, where the flesh ruled but the species declined.

So it was: the music played and the people clapped. And the people danced and things were good for a while in the evenings. In Puerto Vallarta, in a place called Mamma Mia.

Luz María and Danny went there almost every night except when the royalty checks were late coming from Danny's New York agent. In that case they'd lie around their grubby little place down on Madero and drink cheap tequila and screw their heads off, which was sometimes even better than listening to Willie and Lobo. Or maybe something like Willie and Lobo — tight and practiced and wild all at the same time. After living with Danny for two years, and starting even before that, Luz had willingly shed most of the old strictures and hangups of village life, including Catholicism. That wasn't easy,

9

but once it was done, it was done, and done full and pure and forever. That's what Danny believed, or wanted to believe. Made things easier for him, thinking that way.

As Danny said once, speaking with the kind of certainty coming from a ragged blend of drink and experience, there's absolutely nothing like a twenty-two-year-old Mexican woman who's gotten herself liberated and opens up and starts screaming for Jesus Christ to save her immortal Catholic essence while doing every single thing standing in direct contradiction with her words and really meaning she hopes Jesus won't take her now at this moment — maybe later, but not now — not now, with her body sweated and her head tossing from side to side on the pillow and her slim, brown legs waving in the air or draped over the shoulders of a gringo — Danny Pastor, in this case — who's doing his best to put her headlong through the adobe at bed's end and making other superior efforts at seeing she at least spends time in purgatory, if she lucks out at all.

Anyway, on a soft, hot night in 1993, when the sewer system was having its own troubles south of the Río Cuale, Danny and Luz drifted up from Madero to hear Willie and Lobo. But the sound system in Mamma Mia wasn't working up to expectations. That's what Lobo claimed and got sullen about it. After a while Willie started saying that, too. So Willie and Lobo took a long break and went to work on it, broken speaker or some such thing. Luz and Danny walked down the street, dodging tourists and sailors who'd come off an American military ship anchored in the harbor.

For no reason other than doing it, Danny pulled Luz into a hangout called El Niño. El Niño had big wooden shutters that swung open on two sides, along the front where you could look west across Paseo Díaz Ordaz through exhaust fumes and see the sunset on Banderas Bay, and also on the south side looking down on Calle Aldama, where street merchants held up fake silver bracelets to the tourists sitting in El Niño because the guide books said that's where tourists ought to go at sundown.

In the corner of the main room was a particular table where you could put your back against the wall and sweep the room and see who came in, who was walking along Aldama on your left and what was happening out on Ordaz. On the night in question here, with the bar crowded and people talking louder than conditions called for, that special table was occupied by a guy with neatly combed, medium-length silver hair. He was

11

wearing a blue denim shirt and khakis and sitting by himself, drinking a Pacífico with lime. Had a photographer's vest folded over and lying on the windowsill next to him.

Luz and Danny found two seats at the bar and were drinking straight tequila shots with lime plus the usual salt. Danny was talking to the bartender about fish and sun and passing days, while Luz María moved her hand along his thigh — sometimes a little higher when she thought nobody was watching. The touch of Luz María's hand along his leg — and sometimes a little higher — got Danny thinking maybe they ought to stumble back down to Madero and get crazy with love when he noticed the guy at the corner table reach under his vest on the windowsill. Nothing too unusual about that. Later on, Danny couldn't remember why he was paying attention to the man or, for that matter, to anything at all except what Luz was doing along his leg.

Smooth and easy, but quick at the same time, the man checked the room, then lifted the vest a little. Had a gun under the fold, some kind of automatic pistol with a noise suppressor on it. Nobody was watching this except Danny, far as he could tell, since a mime was doing his thing across the street on the Malecón, the cement promenade along the sea, while a mariachi band was playing just behind the mime and sending out a high decibel count for thirty yards in all directions. Everybody was concentrating on the show, including the waiters, while the bartender was tending to someone down the line. But Danny Pastor was staring at this guy with silver hair, like he couldn't believe what was going on was going on and sometimes still can't believe what happened actually did happen when he thinks back on it.

Up came the vest a little more, the gun still mostly covered, and the man's hand jumped three times. No sound that Danny could hear over the mariachis. Just a slight bounce of his hand when he fired. He folded the vest double, stuffed it in a knapsack sitting on the floor by his chair, and looked around. After scanning the room one more time, the man got up and laid out a ten-peso bill, then made his way through the tables and went down the front steps to the street.

While Danny was sitting there temporarily immobilized and feeling like he'd just watched a short instructional film on audacity, which ended without being finished, all hell broke loose out on Ordaz, the mariachis cycling down a little at a time as they figured out something had happened. First one trumpet peeled off, then two of the violins, then the second trumpet stopped, and so on, until they ground down raggedylike and out of tune. They were all looking south along the street, and people were running along the Malecón in the same direction as the band was looking.

Danny slid off his stool, the bartender asking, *"Qué pasa?"* Danny said he didn't know what was happening but that he was going to find out. He walked over to the table where the shooter had been sitting, leaned across it, and looked out in the street. People were crowded around a green Nissan sedan, and he couldn't see anything, so he went down the stairs of El Niño and out on Ordaz.

An American naval officer was lying on the cobblestones, his body twitching and blood coming from a neck wound. Danny, gut tensed, walked past the officer, glancing down at him then quickly away. He went over to the Nissan, stepped on the back bumper and looked over the crowd. Two Mexicans in white short-sleeves and white pants were holding snub-nosed .38s in both hands, pointing them at the sky while they sweated buckets and looked all around with a kind of strange, crazy fear in their eyes. A heavyset gringo in gray slacks and a resorty shirt was lying face up, with the bottom half of him on the street and the upper half on four steps leading from the street up to the

Malecón. Dead center in the gringo's chest was a dark wet spot and a pencil-size slice on his left temple where a bullet had grazed him was oozing red, and he was not moving even the tiniest muscle from what Danny could tell.

Danny went back inside and told Luz and the bartender what he'd seen, mentioning also he didn't think it was a good place to be hanging around in general, not even for a minute and time to finish their drinks since the *policía* were arriving in waves of sirens and confusion. He figured they'd be up in the bar pretty soon, hassling everybody's ass, and he was also thinking he might've been the only one who saw anything, so he hustled Luz María out the back door and over to Morales, heading south toward their place on Madero.

Danny was holding Luz's hand and pulling her along pretty fast. She was half running to keep up with him and asking what was going on, why he was hurrying this way. Probably some kind of premonition, but for reasons that weren't clear to him, he wasn't ready to tell her the whole story, that he'd seen the hit. All she knew was some kind of shooting had taken place. She didn't know Danny had seen the shooter do it and that he was pretty sure he'd been the only

15

one who saw it.

After a few blocks, Danny slowed down and Luz decided an ice cream was necessary. They bought her a cone and walked another block. When they got to El Rondo, little joint with a three-stool bar and four tables, Danny said he needed a drink. Felipe poured him a double tequila and said it was too goddamn hot even for this time of the year and if the goddamn rains would come, things would cool down a little. Danny nodded and wiped his face with a paper napkin.

Luz was licking her blackberry cone, Danny watching her pink tongue circle the mound of ice cream. She watched him watching her and started moving her tongue slow around the ice cream and over the top of it, then put her mouth on it and sucked a little, keeping her eyes on his all the while she was doing these things. She sat back and licked the ice cream from her lips, taking her time and grinning at Danny.

Felipe, who was noticing this unhurried dance toward later-on ecstasy, patted his face with a bar rag and looked at Danny. Danny shook his head and gave Felipe a grin and shrug, still trying to put together what he'd seen fifteen minutes earlier. And shivering inside when he pulled the images up, in the way of remembering a dream you say you don't want to remember but keep remembering anyway because terror has its own fascination, if it's once or twice removed from your own reality. Once or twice removed — terror, that is — until it slow crawls over the transom of your life and pauses there for a moment, looking around for you, eyes bright hard and caring not for your transient joys and sorrows, tongue casting about for your scent.

Movement out on the rim of his left eye, and Danny turned slightly. The man carrying a tan knapsack hesitated at the door to Felipe's before coming inside. Silverish hair and khaki pants. And light blue eyes, maybe gray blue, looking as if they'd seen to the end of things and back. Kind of dead eyes, but with a flicker of something far back inside, like a flashlight coming toward you through the dark from a long way off. Danny's heart seemed not to be working at that moment.

The shooter eased onto a chair, nodded to Felipe. "Tequila, *por favor*."

Luz was looking at the shooter. So was Danny, but trying to appear as if he weren't. Still, he couldn't help glancing at the knapsack the man put under the table five feet away, thinking the two of them, he and the shooter, were the only ones who knew what

17

was in there, but believing the shooter didn't know he knew. And what was in there was the worst kind of bad you could imagine. Danny ordered another double while Luz chewed her cone down to nothing and stared at the shooter in the direct, impertinent way she had when she was curious about something or somebody.

After drinking half his tequila in one swallow, the shooter lit a Marlboro and looked straight at Danny. He was older than he'd seemed when Danny had watched him in El Niño, maybe in his middle fifties or a little more. Dark circles under his eyes, the kind coming with age or from worrying too much or from not getting enough sleep too many nights in a row.

"Buenas noches," the shooter said, lifting his drink up an inch or two in a miniature salute. Gave Danny half a smile, hard smile though.

Danny nodded, said the same thing back to him, working at keeping his voice steady and feeling some bit of a thing coming around in his mind and swimming in there kind of eel-like, more than just hazy shadows yet still not formed in any recognizable way. But it had to do with writing and making money from writing. Maybe the first real money since *Chicago Underground* had come out six

18

years ago. After that, it had been downhill to here, and *here* was beginning to lack a certain charm.

Following *Chicago Underground*, the recollections of an ace reporter, he'd turned to fiction. His first novel, *All the Boys Who Ever Were*, had shown its face in 1989 and fallen on it. "Naive and self-congratulatory; intrepid young journalists in search of truth, regardless of the cost to themselves," said one critic. Another sliced even harder: "However much journalists might like to think of themselves as serious writers, there is, or should be, a rather profound difference between fiction and journalism (though one must admit that difference is becoming more and more indistinguishable). Nonetheless, whatever Mr. Pastor's credentials as a newspaper reporter may be, he certainly is not a novelist and should return forthwith to what he apparently does best — reporting."

As the checks from his agent thinned down to survival money, Danny kept telling Luz and the dross down at Las Noches, where the gringo would-bes and might-have-beens and were-at-one-times hung out and devastated their livers, that he had five or six good ideas under way. What he had and knew he had was rubbish, tales already told a hundred times over and nothing to separate his telling

19

of them from what'd already been said. But he was thinking, not too clearly, and more at the level of instinct than conscious thought, there might be a hell of a story in all this if he could just figure out how to bend it the right way. Get the story, then turn the virulent bastard over to the cops. Perfect: Danny gets rich, Luz is happy, the shooter hangs for his indecencies, and . . . the goddamn critics get it shoved up their noses.

The shooter helped Danny along, or maybe pushed him along, as Danny came to think of it later on.

"I'm looking for a ride up to the border . . . know anyone going that way? I'm willing to pay well for a lift." He was speaking English with pretty good diction, a slow and almost lazy cadence to his voice, keeping his words quiet enough so Felipe couldn't hear. Didn't matter, since Danny was pretty sure Felipe didn't understand English anyway.

"That's a long haul," Danny said, shoving his hands underneath his thighs and sitting hard on them to hold down what might have evolved into a noticeable shake. He looked down at his feet and could see the third toe of his left foot peeking at him through a hole in his sneakers. "Three, three and a half hard days, depending on where you're headed."

He glanced at the shooter. "Most people

fly down here except for truckers and those who have long-term rentals or own houses."

Danny was sweating even more than the evening called for, but nobody seemed to notice. The shooter kept one foot against his knapsack, knowing that way where it was all the time and keeping close track of it. A taxi horn honked twice in the street, and a group of tourists went by Felipe's door, a male voice shouting, "Are you sure this's the right way to Pizza Joe's?"

"Danny has Ford Bronco named Vito." Luz had finished her cone and moved into the conversation, smelling money. She knew they were short, and Luz liked margaritas and going uptown to hear Willie and Lobo and eating lobster at a beach restaurant up the coast in Bucerías. The shooter looked at her; lots of men looked at Luz. She was turned toward him, fine, slim legs crossed and running out from under her lavender dress, the hem of which had worked its way above her knees, wheat-colored sandal hanging from only one toe with silver nail polish on it.

"Who's Danny?"

Luz poked her finger against Danny's arm. "This Danny." She was grinning and speaking pidgin English, which she did sometimes, even though she handled English just about perfectly when she felt like it. Danny signaled

Felipe for another double shot.

The shooter waved off a mosquito buzzing around his right ear, looked at Danny. "You interested in giving me a lift up there, to the border? Say, Laredo or Brownsville, maybe farther west?" Slow, easy words, as if he didn't care when he might get to the border or if he got there at all.

"Not particularly. If I were, I'd charge a hell of a lot more than a first-class ticket on Mexicana would cost." Pretty good, Danny was thinking. A little cagey, showing lack of interest, but still leaving the door open, slowly getting back some of the old confidence from his killer journalism years. Do it the way you did when you were courting the Chicago mob and getting the dope for *Chicago Underground*, making them think they were tough, practical guys who grew up on the scramble while the carriage trade was going off to college. You've handled big dicks before, and the shooter comes off as an easygoing country boy compared to the Chicago wiseguys. Not too smart, either, shooting from the window of a crowded bar. The Chicago kids would have done it in the back on a dark street and ridden the evening train afterward. Danny — Danny boy — get up and get on the high wire and walk it. Walk the wire, concentrate on the other end and

22

don't look down.

The shooter finished his drink, smiled again in that something less than genuine way of his. "I don't like airplanes, never have. Friend dropped me off here from his sailboat. How much?" Now he was concentrating on Luz and her legs or the sandal dangling expectantly from her toe, or some or all of that.

Danny sank back a little. This wasn't working out quite the way he'd expected. He wasn't sure what he'd expected, but this didn't seem to be it. He was feeling somehow he ought to be more in control of the plot, yet the shooter seemed to be moving things along at his own pace. But there was something here worth the telling, something that could bring in some real money and a first-class piece of writing to boot. Danny didn't know much about Mexican law, but in the States this would be called aiding and abetting. If he hauled this guy's tail up to Laredo or wherever, would he be getting himself in serious trouble? Probably, but only if he actually knew the shooter had done something . . . which he did know.

On the other hand, a writer's got to take risks sometime, especially when you're short and might have to take some kind of real job if things don't pick up. Sit around on your can down at Las Noches and nothing happens. *Rolling Stone* would jump at this stuff if he did it as a Hunter Thompson gonzo kind of piece, or maybe it could be serialized in *Esquire* for ten grand and turned into a novel later on. Maybe a film option, too. Call it fiction or write it under a pseudonym. Or make up stuff and pass it off as true, call it "new journalism."

Danny's agent was good at figuring out those details. He could hear her saying, "Go for it, Danny boy; this jerk's nothing more than offal for the great American sausage machine called publishing. What're you going to do with your remaining days, follow all the bullshit dictums of the careful life? Keep your hands in the boat, stay away from the road? Get a do-it-yourself will kit, have a V-8? A buck's a buck, take 'im down. Besides, it'll help with your support payments to Janice and little Robbie, which I understand you're not making at the present time and better start making if you're ever thinking about coming out of Mexico and joining the American parade again."

Something popped inside. "Three thousand American, plus expenses. Fifteen hundred up front." Danny figured it was an absolute ripoff price, making it seem he wasn't all that anxious to go north.

The shooter didn't even blink. "Done.

When can we leave?"

Caught on the stagger, Danny waited a second or two before answering, feeling his mind trying to make decisions without any help from him. Brain sent message to mouth, mouth talked. "Day or two. The Bronco needs a little work."

And while he was saying this out loud in a lurch toward high chance, he was also saying to himself, Back up, back down, get out and go home. Still, events have a force of their own once they're under way, and it was too late, somehow. Somehow, too late. Confusing: tequila, money, Luz, back to *el Norte* and better things . . . no . . . yes . . . shit, what am I doing?

"Would an extra two thousand plus twenty-five hundred front-end money get me a departure in the next couple of hours? I have to meet someone in Dallas." Some part of Danny's mind was working on the shooter's accent, trying to place it. Mostly nondescript midwestern, with a hint of East Coast here and there on certain words.

Somewhere in the middle of a tunnel closing behind him, Danny Pastor was looking backward and going forward at the same time. Mouth again: "The Mexican highways are messy, gets long and lonely out there, especially at night. Things can go wrong."

The shooter thought for a moment, then spoke slowly with an interior smile underneath his words. "Sounds like an overall description of life to me. What's the problem, bad fellows?"

"Maybe. Break down and the local thugs who have a general dislike for gringos might try to beat on us. Word is, bandidos are back in business on Fifteen up north and also around Durango, east in the mountains. On top of that, the *federales* can think up about a million reasons to give you trouble, even if you aren't involved in any trouble to start with. They operate as their own law, more or less. Hard to tell 'em from the bandidos. Mexican law descends from the Napoleonic Code, not English common law, so habeas corpus is not part of doing business down here. They get you in jail and figure you'll just sit there for life or until someone from the States sends a few thousand in bribe money to get you out."

The shooter toyed with his empty shot glass, tilted it up, and looked at the bottom. "Well, there's two of us. We can watch each other's backs, can't we?"

He glanced up at Danny, who wasn't sure whether the question was rhetorical or required an answer, decided on the former, and focused momentarily on where the shooter was fiddling with his shot glass — the little finger on his left hand was missing.

In any case, by the easy way he'd said it, the shooter obviously wasn't worried about village thugs or bandidos, maybe not even *federales* or anyone else who might jump up and get in his way. He'd just cracked some important-looking gringo plus a naval officer for whatever reason, and he was sitting there with that hard little smile of his, like the whole thing was an evening stroll along the Malecón.

Danny was still considering a fast tunnel backward toward the light of where he was an hour ago, toward recommended and sensible boundaries. Alternatives: Stay in Puerto Vallarta and ride Luz María's warm and willing body into another thousand sunsets, get some real work done on another book while waiting for the next royalty check that'd be less than the previous one. Good choice, if low risk and even lower money were the criteria.

Or, haul ass off into the Mexican night with a killer who might just put a pencil-size hole behind your right ear somewhere out on the road. At that level, bad choice. Still, five thousand for the ride plus another ten for the serial rights plus a book would sum to plenty of long, easy nights of Willie and

Lobo, not to mention Luz, who could get especially willing and somewhere on the far side of enthusiastic with lobster and drink swirling around in her soft brown tummy. And maybe a few dollars up to Chicago for Janice and little Robbie, show good intentions and that sort of thing. Besides, Danny figured the shooter had no quarrel with him, and professional hit men don't hit anybody they don't have to. That's one of their survival tactics, which is something Danny knew from his newspapering days on the streets of Chicago.

So there was the business of money — the compulsions of greed or necessity, usually indistinguishable — plus the tequila in Danny's head and the consequent upward slope of his risk curve toward imprudence. Not to mention ill-considered wed to misguided and penny wise cum imbecility. Later on, Danny Pastor would know Proust had it right: "It is always thus, impelled by a state of mind which is destined not to last, that we make our irrevocable decisions."

Some years before, Janice, Danny's first and only wife, had said it differently, "Danny, make it a personal rule never to make decisions when you're drinking. They're always bad ones. Tattoo that rule on top of your thumb so you'll see it when you lift the glass."

As they used to say, and put on T-shirts now, tequila has four stages:

> I'm rich,
>> I'm beautiful,
>>> I'm bulletproof,
>>>> I'm invisible.

Danny was at stage three and climbing when he decided to take the shooter north, toward wherever it is men go when they're out of their minds or in need of money . . . which amount to the same thing most of the time.

Back Routes

Danny's '68 Bronco, torn seats and modified to three-on-the-floor with a choice of either two- or four-wheel drive, was boxy and high set and pretty much a rolling disaster. Standard issue for the expats who hung around beach towns. He'd bought it when he'd first come to Puerto Vallarta three years before, from another gringo down there squandering life. Salt wind and gritty dust had taken the original brown paint, and where you couldn't see primer you saw rust, and where you couldn't see rust you saw holes. After holes, infinity. It was parked under two scraggly almond trees, by the side of the building where Danny and Luz had an apartment on the second floor.

The shooter stared at the Bronco. "Kind of a forlorn old sailor. Think it'll make it to the border?"

"With two days to get it ready I'd say the chances would be pretty good. Pulling out like we are, middle of the night and all, it's anybody's guess. I've got some new plugs and an extra fan belt in the house. I'll bring 'em along.

"Luz, start filling up those empty plastic water jugs we've been saving; we'll probably need to top off the radiator more than once."

"How many miles on this thing called Vito?" The shooter touched one of the Bronco's fenders.

"Engine was replaced in seventy-six. Hundred and twenty-seven thousand on this one."

When the three of them had left El Rondo, Felipe, in a condition of studied lassitude, not to mention squinch eyed and feigning disinterest, was wiping off tables and his face with the same towel. Felipe was getting on, but he hadn't lost his taste for pretty señoritas, and the gringos came and went, leaving young Mexican women behind and in need of counseling or a place to stay. One never knew. He'd gone to the door and watched the rear of the señorita's lavender dress until they'd turned a corner and headed down Juarez, ducking back inside for a moment when the tall man in a blue shirt had turned and glanced at him.

Danny had taken them down darkened back streets, past closed restaurants and tourist markets and small hotels with neon vacancy signs missing a letter or two. Danny and Luz had walked ahead of the shooter, who paused at each street crossing before stepping out and catching up, moving on long, easy strides of the kind that were soundless and a throwback to the veldwalkers who measured their distances by days and lifetimes. Later on, Luz would remark on that, how the tall, thin man hesitated at street crossings, as if he were afraid of being seen, how he covered ground like a big cat, like *el gato* walking soft in a mountain night.

Halfway across the bridge on Insurgentes, they'd gone down stone steps to an island cutting the Río Cuale in two. The island was dark, and a short way along it was a suspension bridge crossing the south half of the river. A drunk had been hanging over the western bridge cable, vomiting into the river. They'd passed around him and cut down Constitución to Madero and the apartment.

In a state of tequila decline, mouth dry and nerves wobbly, Danny Pastor moved around the Bronco, checking tires, aware of the shooter standing a few feet away. Someone was playing a guitar in a nearby building, slightly out of tune and sounding muffled and distant and being just about the perfect launch music for Danny's version of a run to *el Norte*. On a Tuesday night, with tomorrow a work day, it was mostly quiet along Madero, except for a group of people gathered at the end of the block, talking fast and pointing uptown where sirens were going off.

"What else we need?" The shooter was leaning against one of the trees by the Bronco, looking up and down the street, then at Danny.

"I'm not planning on camping out," Danny said. "There're resthouses, hotels, and other things of various stripes in the larger towns along the way. Depends how fancy you want to get. We'll take some food, drinking water, and tools in case Vito decides to get balky. You got a hat? The sun's a cannibal during the day."

The shooter gave his knapsack an easy slap. "Everything I need is in here."

Danny was pretty sure that was as true and profound as language got.

"Where do we pick up the food and water?"

"It's a little this side of eleven-thirty. There's a couple of small stores on Insurgentes that stay open late. We'll get some things on our way out. You sure must be in a hurry." Danny wished he hadn't said that, about the shooter being in a hurry. Not that there was anything wrong with it — a little off-the-cuff remark that might be expected — but it didn't need to be said. Don't say any more than you have to say. Stay back, stay quiet, watch and listen.

"Not that much of a hurry. I finished up some business here tonight, and I'm restless. Got to see a man in Dallas in a few days, like I said, but I should make it all right. I thought if we got under way pronto, it might give us time to take a more scenic route on the way up."

"Mister . . . hell, I don't even know your name. Mine's Danny Pastor."

"You're right, not very mannerly of me. Peter Schumann, here."

Danny didn't believe him and went under the hood, checking the distributor wires, adjusting the carburetor. "Like I started out to say before we got into introductions, *any* way up to the border is the scenic route." His voice was reverberant in the closed space between hood and motor. He turned the carburetor screw, and the engine revved up for a moment before he leveled it back down.

"You've obviously never seen the Mexican highway system. Not bad in parts, pretty raw other places, holes in the pavement that'll break an axle if I hit one in the dark, cattle standing in the middle of the road when you come around a corner. At night a whole lot of the Mexicans drive with their lights off for reasons that've never been all that clear to me. It's a mess. Decided where you want me to drop you off, which border town?"

"Still thinking about it. Got a map?"

"Damn!" Danny had skinned two knuckles on his right hand yanking out the oil stick in the dark. He straightened up, wiping his hands on a greasy cloth. "There's a good Mexican road map under the driver's seat. Little torn and smudged, but still readable."

The shooter pulled a small flashlight out of a side pocket in his knapsack and unfolded the map.

Vito turned over, rough and noisy, billowing blue smoke into the black night, bringing down a curse on Danny's head from the apartment building next door. He shut off the engine just as Luz stumbled out of the house with a gallon water jug in each hand, long-billed fishing cap on her head and sweater over her shoulder. She'd changed into old jeans and a white T-shirt with "Puerto Vallarta Squeeze" printed in faded green letters on the front and featuring two halves of a lime lying over the appropriate parts of her chest along with what was supposed to be a rendering of lime juice dribbling down between those parts.

"Wait a minute," Danny said. "You don't think for a minute you're going along." Risking his own hide for a story was one thing. Bringing Luz under that cloud was something else again.

She nodded. "I want to see *el Norte.*"

"Luz, we're not going to the United States. I'm dropping Mr. Schumann off at a border town and heading straight back here."

She looked up at Danny in a way that promised double helpings of whatever she could invent that was new and different and depraved, if he'd just take her on this voyage. That kind of skin-soft persuasion wasn't good enough, not this time.

Still, explaining why she couldn't come along was going to be tough. For all she knew, the shooter was just some crazy gringo who didn't like airplanes and had business in Dallas. If Danny told her about him, she'd know something she didn't need to know, something that could hurt her if the shooter found out or if the *federales* started asking her questions for whatever reason. The *federales* had ways of getting information when they wanted it, especially from a woman.

On the other hand, if this was simply a delivery job to the border, there was no reason why she shouldn't go. And if Danny said absolutely not, no way, she'd piss and moan and cry and maybe just take off somewhere, the way she threatened to do whenever they had a serious scrap. On top of that, she'd tell everyone they knew about this safari into the high North. It wouldn't take overriding

36

genius for someone to pull the shooting to-gether with Danny leaving in the middle of the night accompanied by a strange gringo who had to get to the border fast and didn't like airplanes. Even the *policía* could figure that one out.

"It's okay with me if she comes along." The shooter studied the map while he talked, face thin and shadow-lit by the flashlight re-flecting off the map. "You drive, she handles food and water and communications problems or whatever, I watch the horizon for bandidos and other perils of the road. It's a nice three-legged stool of mutual support."

"See, it all right with him if I go along."

Shit. Getting complicated, as if it weren't already complicated enough. The shooter had practically invited her, and Danny had no way of explaining why she couldn't come without taking her inside and whispering in her ear. In that case, she'd tear her hair and plead with Danny not to go. The sum of all these little pieces was the shooter would sense something was wrong and maybe do bad things to both of them.

Danny gave it another try, a feeble one. "Luz, the Bronco has only two seats . . . no place for you to sit. The back'll be filled with gear." She'd worked that out already and said she could sit on the sleeping bag and stack the supplies around her.

She went back up the stairs for the sleeping bag and three cans of Pennzoil stashed under the sink. The shooter had to use the bathroom and followed her inside. Somehow, in a way Danny couldn't quite get hold of, the situation was taking on a life of its own. Things had a way of doing that when you hadn't thought them through ahead of time. It was called the *Qué Será, Será* school of planning, the wrinkled blueprint for Danny's life over the last few years when he'd decided, without deciding, to let the tropics have their way with him.

Danny slammed the Bronco's hood and watched Luz come out of the apartment building. She walked over to him, carrying a sleeping bag, a big flashlight, and a small duffel bag of clothes for Danny. An over-weight couple stopped and asked how to find a bus out to the Sheraton. The woman, with blue curled hair underneath a beribboned straw beach hat, spoke with a grating nasality. Danny glanced at their name tags carrying a "Snap-On Tools" logo and suggested they walk down to Insurgentes and find a taxi, easier this time of night. They moved on, complaining to each other about bus service in Mexican towns.

He checked the building's doorway, no sign

of the shooter, then spoke low and hard to Luz. "Don't say *anything* about us being in El Niño tonight or about the shooting. Got that? *Nothing*. I'll explain later." She nodded, obviously confused but trusting him and glad to be going along. The shooter came out of the building's doorway, looking up and down the street as he walked.

They closed up the apartment, piled in the Bronco, and backed onto Madero. Luz burrowed in behind Danny and the shooter, nesting in a mélange of water jugs, cans of motor oil, and other gear.

The shooter handed Danny twenty-five one-hundred-dollar bills.

"That's a lot of cash to be carrying around, particularly in Mexico." Danny was shifting into second and rolling toward Insurgentes.

The shooter took a navy blue ball cap from his knapsack, bent the bill into a half oval, and pulled it low over his eyes.

"I have my quirks. I don't like airplanes, and I don't like traveler's checks or credit cards."

Danny handed the money back to Luz. "Stick this way down inside the sleeping bag. If we get stopped by the *federales* or the judicial police, I'd prefer not to have my pockets bulging with American *dinero*."

He glanced at the shooter. "Aren't you

39

afraid of being rolled, carrying around that much cash?"

The shooter was slowly moving his head back and forth like a radar antenna, scanning the street ahead and both sides of it.

"It's been tried." He spoke in a detached way, as if he were on time-share, concentrating on something else. "Five of the boy-os made a move on me in Manila once."

"What happened?"

"Didn't work out the way they'd planned. Overconfidence will do that to you."

Danny should have listened to those words. Later on and looking back, he was pretty sure the shooter was trying to tell him something, but he'd been concentrating on getting them through the streets and thinking about what this story would do for his wallet *and* his reputation — a whole new rejuvenated Danny Pastor, comeback kid and demon of the talk shows, recipient of literary prizes and hero to right-thinking citizens everywhere.

He'd never realized how tricky it is to know something about somebody and not let them know you know when you're trying to help them for all the wrong reasons. Insurgentes was a bright, major thoroughfare running north through town, eventually tying into other streets and leading toward the airport. The problem was how to get out of town without being noticed and at the same time not be too obvious about it so he didn't tip off the shooter about knowing more than he was supposed to know.

Danny parked the Bronco on a side street near the Río Cuale and went around the corner to a small grocery store on Insurgentes. Fruit, candy bars, cheese, loaf of bread, two gallons of drinking water. And a bottle of Pepto-Bismol, economy size. As he climbed in the Bronco, a truckload of police bounced north along Insurgentes, siren blaring.

"What's all the excitement?" the shooter asked, sounding innocent and only a little curious.

"The hombre tending the store says there's been some kind of shooting over on Ordaz. That's what the sirens and traffic are about. The *federales* probably will be stopping everybody on the highway out, looking at papers, searching cars, and all the rest of that good crap. I'm going to take a back route that's a little rough, but it'll save us a lot of time and hassle." Pretty decent, reasonable explanation. Christ, Danny said to himself, I'm already thinking like a criminal.

"That sort of thing happen often here? Shootings?" The shooter was lying back, seeming to be relaxed, flicking cigarette ashes out the side as they bumped over cobble-

41

stones. But he never stopped looking every-where at once.

"Not very often. Lot of petty stuff, not much heavy violence."

"Who got hit?" Interesting choice of words. Most people would have said "shot" or some-thing along those lines.

"Don't know for sure." Danny swerved to miss a rumbling bus carrying night workers north toward the big tourist hotels. "Appar-ently an American navy officer and some other gringo. Most likely a bar fight."

He couldn't see Luz's face, but she had to be wondering just what the hell he was doing and why he was saying less than he knew. And the bar fight explanation was a little weak, since American naval officers weren't given over to that sort of thing.

Danny took the Bronco into the back streets of Puerto Vallarta. Across the Río Cuale at a shallow spot, through the storage yard of an old foundry, in behind the new Pizza Hut, and down a dirt road where the poorest of the Mexican workers lived, which included most of the locals. He could still hear sirens six blocks west, in the general direction of El Niño. The *policía* and probably the army, maybe even *federales,* were running around like malevolent Keystone Kops, but most of the regular people were turning in for the night. Whatever had happened was none of their business. So what if a couple of rich gringos were down on the cobblestones. If it wasn't bullets, it'd be AIDS or dope or booze. A lot of them came here, running away from something back home and toward a sleazy, inelegant end in the white enclaves of Puerto Vallarta. For the Mexicans it was something to talk about at work tomorrow, but not important in the day-to-day scheme of surviving poverty and feeding the family.

Back down the years, someone had installed a roll bar in the Bronco, and the shooter was hanging on to it with his left hand, smoking Marlboros with the other, knapsack between his feet on the floor and staying quiet. Danny moved along an arroyo in four-wheel drive and suddenly there was Route 200. He stopped short of the highway, let Vito idle, and walked up on the road. A *federale* station sat just north of the airport. They were a mile north of the station, parked in a riverbed, with the traffic looking normal along the highway. If there was a roadblock, which Danny guessed there was, it must have been closer in to the city, probably at the *federale* outpost. The Bronco climbed up the riverbank, rolled over broken glass, and hit the pavement. Danny took it out of four-wheel drive, and they headed toward *el Norte,* windows down and the breeze beginning to dry the sweat on Danny's face and everywhere else.

Danny talked to the shooter without looking at him. "In about an hour I'd like to know which border town you want. If we're heading straight north toward Nogales, I'm going up a coast road for a while. It takes a little longer, but we'll avoid some of the heavy truck traffic around Tepic. Otherwise we'll curl back southeast toward Guadalajara and catch the roads up to Laredo or El Paso or Brownsville."

The shooter's flashlight bounced around as he studied the map. "According to what I'm seeing here, we don't have to make the decision that early. Looks like another east-west road further north. Comes out of Mazatln and heads over to Durango."

"Yeah, but it's a horror story. Some guy once counted the curves between Mazatlán and Durango. Claims there're thirty-three hundred of 'em. Also lots of falling rock up in those mountains, all kinds of small boulders lying on the highway, bandidos on top of that. But it's your nickel."

The shooter said nothing. They blew up the middle of Bucerías and then past the turn-off to Punta de Mita, where Luz and Danny used to swim naked at night and sometimes in the afternoons before Japanese fat cats started in on it with their fences and bull-dozers and condo blueprints.

A little farther north, Luz poked him in the shoulder and shouted over the wind, "Guamúchil." Danny nodded and thought of the little village off in the jungle. A woman in Guamúchil made tortillas the old way, by hand, rice-paper thin and filled with hot salsa. She cooked them on the top of an oil drum cut out and laid over a circle of rocks with a fire underneath. Luz and Danny had gone there once, bought a handful of the tortillas, and walked through the jungle, eating them and sucking on wild limes. Danny had wanted to see a boa constrictor, but they hadn't found any. Boas are hard to get a fix on, that's what someone told him. You have to know their habits and watch the overhead branches.

An hour later Danny pulled off the road a kilometer south of Las Varas. They sat there in darkness, big stars on the other side of the windshield, Vito idling like a slow coffee grinder with teeth missing. He turned the ignition key. Dead quiet except for crickets in the background and the riffle of night breeze around them.

"Which way?"

The shooter was looking at the map again, using his little flashlight. He folded the map, stuck it under the seat, and lit a cigarette. "Let's hold off on the choice for a while. Take that coast road you were talking about, the one with less traffic. We'll talk routes again at Mazatlán. I might want to head up to Sonoyta."

"Where the hell is that?" Danny had never heard of Sonoyta.

"Stay on Fifteen up to Santa Ana, just like you're going to Nogales. At Santa Ana, take Route Two west . . . goes right up to Sonoyta."

"What's the U.S. border town there?"

"Isn't any. Ajo, Arizona, is a little north of the border, Gila Bend's another forty miles past Ajo."

"That's a long way from Dallas, if Dallas is where you're headed."

"Sonoyta, maybe." That's all he said.

Danny started the Bronco, turned left in Las Varas, and took the three of them northwest through the warm Mexican night. He'd hung a radio off the dashboard a year ago and flipped it on now; song he'd heard before was playing. Luz had told him it was based on an old Nahua poem from the days of the Conquistadors:

Nothing remains but flowers
and sad songs

46

Where once there were warriors
and wise men. . . .

The shooter looked out Vito's right side,
into darkness. He looked that way for a long
time, then put a worn desert boot up on the
dash and slouched in his seat, ball cap pulled
even lower than before, as if he were sleeping.
But Danny was pretty sure he wasn't.

Shadowmen

Recoil. Counterpoint. As Danny Pastor shifted the Bronco into third gear, running toward *el Norte* through the blanket-soft night of coastal Mexico, a Learjet 35 climbed out of Andrews Air Force Base through light rain and headed toward cruising altitude. Walter McGrane loosened his seat belt, pulled up the cuff of his safari jacket, and checked his watch: Puerto Vallarta by dawn. He settled back and studied the two men in the club seats opposite him. A never-ending line of them as the years went by, young and hard and confident. Always the same, young and hard and confident, while Walter McGrane just got older. Dressed in jeans and windbreakers, on temporary reassignment from a special ops branch of the army, they drank coffee and talked a language made obscure and privileged by the acronyms of their trade.

Packed in two black duffels lying in the narrow aisle were the tools of that trade. The long guns: M-40A1 sniper rifle fitted with a 10X Unertl telescopic sight; M16A2 high-capacity assault weapon; Remington pump shotgun, full-choked and with seven inches cut from the barrel for close-in work. The sidearms: Smith & Wesson .40-caliber automatics.

Each had a webbed vest with extra clips for the assault weapon and thirty rounds of match-grade hollowpoint ammunition for the sniper rifle, a handheld radio, minibinoculars, compass, canteen, extra pistol magazines, penlight with filter, Mace, camouflage paste, first-aid kit, plastic arm/leg restraints, notebook and pen, a clip-on thermometer for monitoring temperature changes and compensating for their effect on bullet trajectories. Those things, other things, neatly arranged in the vest pockets.

The Lear bucked once, then again, and the men across from Walter McGrane held Styrofoam cups away from their laps, letting coffee slosh over the rims and onto the cabin floor. When the plane had cleared the turbulence and leveled off, McGrane opened his briefcase and unfolded one of several detailed maps of Mexico he'd been given at his briefing two hours ago. Son of a bitch, this would have to happen the day before his thirty-second wedding anniversary. Not that he cared much about anniversaries of any kind, but his wife did, and he'd have fires to put out at home for the next six months and be reminded the following year of how he'd missed the last anniversary. All because of Clayton Price.

As with all wars, Vietnam had produced its share of crazies, and now Clayton Price, a.k.a. Peter Schumann and other handles, had become one of those who'd apparently gone over to rogue. Never would have guessed it, that's what had been said at the briefing. Never would have guessed it about Clayton Price, but then they were all time bombs, particularly the sniper teams — the years of training to kill, and the killing itself, the flattened value structures and suppressed emotions necessary to carry out their work. Some could be flat and cold for only so long, living as they did with the recollections of blood and brain shots clearly monitored down the long lens of a twenty-power spotting scope.

Walter McGrane studied the map and wondered which way Clayton Price would run. North probably. Or maybe he'd bolt for the jungles of Central America. Price understood jungles as well as anyone and far better than most. He'd been one of the best shooters who'd ever worked for them, one of the best who'd ever lived, strange and distant, with more patience than a boulder. That's why he'd been called "Tortoise" in his Vietnam years, slow and methodical and patient. Somebody once said if Clayton Price slowed down any more, he'd be moving backward. That is, until the right moment came and he instantly evolved into something more like a snake. Reptilian, in any case, whether he was waiting or striking.

That's what was said about Clayton Price when he was young and fast. But it was generally agreed now that he was getting old, too old and out-of-date, thinking too much and asking questions about things he didn't need to know, losing his edge. The Covert Operations Unit had stopped using him five years ago except in certain circumstances where an extra hand was needed.

Old and out-of-date. Out of round. Out of step and style, out of order and out of tune. Clayton Price — Tortoise — and Nightingale and Centipede and Broadleaf, a few others. The shadowmen, operating in the information penumbra cast by governments when moments of secrecy are required and things need to be accomplished without the rest of the world knowing about them. Well, scratch Centipede. He'd never made it out of some godforsaken Middle Eastern place last year — South Yemen, the rumors said — land mine or gunned down by laser-controlled Gatling as he cut his way through concertina wire. Whatever got him, it was something metallic and forever and final. That's what Clayton Price had heard. And political repercussions afterward; that's what Walter McGrane knew for sure.

The radio Danny Pastor had slung from the dash kept on playing: warriors and wise men, flowers and sad songs, Mexican night rolling by. Luz María was awake, saying nothing. Clayton Price was awake and thinking about Centipede, about the time they'd gone into Ecuador as a team and taken out three revolutionaries who were using the drug trade to finance leftist efforts on behalf of a better world. That was damn near the end for both of them. If it hadn't been for the gutsy pilot in the old C-47, it would have been the end. He'd landed on grassed-over asphalt and slowed only enough to let them run alongside and climb in the cargo door, as if they were hopping a freight. Tortoise and Centipede, tight-lipped at first, then laughing and giving each other a high-five when they'd made it over the Andes. Insertion was hard enough, extraction was where it always got real close. Like now, in Mexico.

His shoulder pressed against the Bronco's door as Danny Pastor took Vito around a hard, left-bending curve. A long, strange life, it had been that all right. From the beginning, it seemed, promised to the field of battle. Way back in another time, he might have been something else, a sailor on one of Cook's voyages or a mountain man in the high evergreens.

Mountain men . . . from the Park Slope area of Brooklyn, you could see Manhattan across the East River, and on foggy days the towers resembled mountains; that's how he'd imagined it when he was young. He'd sat in the bay window of his parents' fourth-floor walk-up, three floors above an Italian restaurant taking up the whole bottom floor, and had thought about mountain men. He'd read about them in a library book and after that wanting to be one and having the freedom to go where the wind took you and coming back only when you felt like it. No buses, no subways, no school, none of that.

The day he'd left Park Slope for good was low hung and dark, foggy a little, and the towers had looked like mountains again. He'd stood there looking at them across the East River getting ice along its edges, thinking it might be the last time he'd see those mountains, probably for sure the last he'd see of them from this window. He was going to Minnesota, and he wasn't certain if there were mountains out there or not, didn't think so. Lakes, though, that's what his mother said. She'd told him that a week before, exactly a month to the day after his father had pulled out, leaving Clayton and her alone.

When Clayton had asked, "Why'd Dad leave us?" his mother replied, "Elmer just felt closed in, I guess." She'd been all weepy and slumped over when she'd said it.

Clayton was the youngest of five children, the other four gone and paying their way, and his parents had been old by parent standards when he'd come along, unexpected and unwelcome.

"We didn't plan on Clayton," his mother had said once to a friend of hers and not aware Clayton could hear them talking. "There were things we wanted to do, and they didn't include another child. My God, four are enough to raise in this world."

"Land sakes, yes." The other woman had nodded in fast agreement, sweeping her hand as if she were brushing away unwanted children. "I should think so. We stopped after three. Nobody needs a caboose these days."

His mother had sat him down and told him what was for sure and what had to be done. "Clayton, I've found a job at Landowski's Cleaners over on Fourteenth, but I can't make enough to take care of us both. Your grandparents out in Ely say it's all right if you come and live with them for a while. It's real nice there, lots of lakes and woods. You'll be happier out of the city. I'll find a smaller place I can afford and send along a little money if I can."

Clayton Price had looked at his mother, blue eyes running toward gray looking straight at her. His father was gone, his mother was sending him away. . . . "We didn't plan on Clayton. . . . There were things we wanted to do." He'd understood, in a way. She already looked old at fifty-two, as old as his grandparents looked in the photograph on the bureau in her room, and they looked older than Jim Bowie's grave.

Clayton may have understood . . . kind of, why his parents hadn't wanted him, how he'd screwed up their plans. He may have understood . . . kind of, but he'd been only ten and a caboose at that, and Ely, Minnesota, had seemed forever out there someplace.

Margaret Price and her unexpected youngest son had ridden the train to Manhattan. There she'd put Clayton on a bus headed west. November 29, 1952, that's when it was, and snowing heavy by late afternoon. Margaret Price always remembered afterward how hard it had been snowing when Clayton got into the Greyhound. Army had defeated

55

Navy 7–0 earlier in the day, Ike was going to be the new president, the French Union forces in Vietnam were doing pretty well and looking as if they'd stopped the march of communism right in its tracks.

The bus had rolled out of the Port Authority Terminal and Margaret Price was waving to Clayton on that day and not able to see him very well behind the steamed-up windows. Clayton Price had eight dollars in his pocket, and Ely, Minnesota, had looked like a long way down the road. He'd wondered again for about the millionth time why his father left when and how he did, just pulling out that way, and that was something nobody ever knew.

"The bus drivers'll help you, Clayton, and your grandfolks'll meet you in Duluth." His mother had said those words somewhere around twenty times that one afternoon before the Greyhound closed its big door with a sigh and headed for a far place.

Clayton had wiped at the steamy window beside him, making circular motions with his mitten on the glass, trying to see his mother one more time. She'd stood there and was hard to see in all the smoke from a lot of buses and on the other side of a window that was dirty on the outside and which Clayton couldn't get perfectly free of steam on the inside no matter how hard and fast he'd wiped it. People were already carrying Christmas packages, hurrying through the weather and passing in front of and behind Margaret Price in her black cloth coat and faded orange scarf. Big wheels turning and Margaret Price running then alongside the bus on the wet street with her purse hanging over her left arm and flopping out there all the while she ran. And Clayton reading her lips with which she was saying, "I love you," but he didn't believe it then and didn't later on and never would after that day.

When he'd finished boot camp at Parris Island in 1960, both Margaret and Elmer Price had come down for the ceremonies. He hadn't invited them, but his grandmother had written Margaret and said Clayton had joined the marines partly because his teeth needed a lot of fixing and the government said they'd fix his teeth if he joined up. His parents had gotten back together a year after he'd left Park Slope but never said anything about him coming back there and sending instead some money to Ely each month to help out with his board.

His head had been shaved close for the ceremonies, and he'd received a special award for marksmanship. A younger Clayton Price had been able to hit a jackrabbit on the run in heavy brush by the time he left Ely, could do it with a .22-long rifle bullet. He hadn't cared much for shooting at stationary targets the way they had in boot camp, and it wasn't hard measured up against what you had to do in the woods, particularly for Clayton Price. Some people can draw faces or make pool balls dance to any tune they want right from the start; others can think through mathematics and paint in watercolors. Clayton Price could handle guns and eventually out-shot twenty-six hundred other marksmen at the National High-Power Rifle Championship at Camp Perry, Ohio. He did that later on in the early sixties, did it shooting at a target a thousand yards out where the bulls-eye looked like a pinhead down his scope.

His parents had come up to him after the ceremony and all full of pride and saying how fine he looked in his uniform. Clayton hadn't smiled, not even a flicker of one, and he hadn't been trying to hold it back or anything, it just hadn't been there for these people from another time, from a different planet or an-other world, was how he thought of them back then and still did ever after in the times out in front of him. But the marines in ad-dition to fixing his teeth had taught him some-thing about being a gentleman, so he'd shaken hands with both of them and hadn't done any more than just that all the while his mother was standing on her tiptoes and kissing his cheek and having her picture taken with him. Said then he had to go, even though he hadn't gone anywhere except back to the barracks, where he'd cried a little over seeing those people from another world again and knowing then he'd never go near them, not one more time in his life. Also knowing the best way to go from there on out was not to count on anyone ever again or even to care for anyone again or let anyone care for you.

And a few years later, dawn and warm rain falling on leaves and grass, mist above the rice paddies. Twelve hours in the "hide" with gnats around your face and ants crawling in your ears and under your clothes . . . leeches hanging on to you . . . mosquitoes biting and you can't swat them away, no movement allowed. Becoming part of the landscape. Estimating windage by the feel of it on your face and the bend of grass five hundred yards out, watching heat waves to get a sense of how the bullet will ride. Living for a week on nothing but water and basic C-rations — peanut butter, jelly, cheese, and crackers. Four more killing days to Christmas, as a major had said before the chopper took off last night.

Lying there, concentrating, looking for a movement of brown or green in a wall of brown and green. Scanning the natural lines of drift where people tend to walk or rest. Mornings and evenings are best. Charlie's just waking up or tired and careless after a day's work.

The beat of your heart against the earth, the smell of solvent residue coming off your rifle bolt, a flat-shooting Remington 700 with a Redfield nine-power scope.

"There he is," your spotter whispers. "The hamburger in the door, epaulets and clean uniform, binoculars. NVA colonel."

Officers: Always look for the clean uniform, the binoculars, the one with a radio man close by. Dumb bastard's standing in the door of a hut, yawning.

Check your body position and scope picture.

"I make it eight five zero yards," you whisper.

"Eight fifty, eight seventy-five," your spotter whispers back.

It all seems kind of . . . kind of dreamlike. Your teacher, White Feather, calls it his "bubble," going into a place of concentration and focus so clear that it becomes a universe of its own where nothing and no one can intrude.

Check again: the bend of grass, the heat waves.

Wait for the flattest part of your breathing cycle.

Control the trigger pull, the follow-through.

The recoil against your shoulder, and on the other side of the valley, a man jolts back into the darkness of a hut.

Your spotter gives you a thumbs-up, and the two of you begin a reverse crawl down your escape route.

The world of Clayton Price.

A strange world, and a long, strange life, aloneness mostly, loneliness sometimes. Never a woman for any amount of time. Nothing like the one riding close behind him, the one he could smell in the compressed space of a Bronco called Vito when they slowed and the breeze no longer blew away the pleasant mix of perfume and sweat coming off her. He straightened in his seat and glanced back. Luz María was looking at him.

In the Learjet hammering southwest, different smells. The distinct, unalloyed scents of coffee and gun oil. Walter McGrane glanced up when he heard the soft click of a rifle bolt. One of the men across from him was examining the sniper rifle. He watched

61

the man work the bolt, checking over the tool of graceful agony that could have been a candidate for an award in contemporary design, curving metal and angular parts machined to a level of precision usually reserved for fine watches. The man, machined to precision like the rifle and known to him only as Weatherford, ran a soft cloth along the barrel as if he were touching a woman.

The rifle, forty-four inches long and weighing a little over fourteen pounds with its scope, was chambered for a match-grade 7.62, 173-grain bullet. One second after being fired, the bullet would hit the center of a man's chest at a thousand yards, over a half mile away, every time, in the hands of a skilled marksman, and the men across from Walter McGrane were skilled. Sometime in the next few days, if things went well and the Mexican government stayed out of their way, the reticles on the sniper's scope would lie across the chest of Clayton Price, who would never hear the sound that killed him.

Walter McGrane didn't like going after one of their own. He didn't much like any of this anymore. But so be it and so it lay. He was a field man by his own preference, and he'd been ordered to do it by the Pure Intelligence office boys, the suits, the idiot theoreticians, "espiocrats," as le Carré or somebody had called them. Those who'd never used a dead drop in Bucharest, had never worn goggles in the blowing dust of Algeria while a jeep climbed rocky outcrops, had never done a goddamned thing except go to school. Had no idea what the field was like, the calm and concentration on the face of a man such as Broadleaf when you were putting him out in some bloody middle-of-nowhere to do a job. On paper, everything looked good. In the dust and smoke out where it all happened, there was always the human factor, the Clayton Prices going off the path and screwing up the neat calculations and impeccable logic.

By their own choices, the shadowmen marched in a narrow path of rules and instruction, and any deviation meant things would come to an end for them. Everyone knew that and accepted it; some walked off the path anyway for reasons they alone might understand but probably couldn't articulate. Years from now, or even tomorrow, the men across from Walter McGrane might go off the path without warning from their actions or words. Fortunately, most of them did not and retired to obscure places where they planted gardens and lived with their images of blood and brains and work carried out for reasons they'd never been told.

All of them, the scout-snipers, were hand-picked. The best were farm boys or other bush-smart kids who spent their growing years in the out-of-doors, where they developed fieldcraft skills and a sharp sense of how nature operates, acquired a sense of belonging to the wild. North country trappers, West Texas deer stalkers, Arkansas squirrel hunters. Excellent noncorrected vision, slow heartbeat. Great physical condition, mental discipline, attention to detail, and, most of all, that thing called patience.

Over the years, Walter McGrane had worked with Centipede and Broadleaf, never with Tortoise. But he'd heard about him, had read the dossier.

PRICE, CLAYTON LEE

. . . as with other scout-snipers, Gunnery Sgt. Price has strong mental stability and patience to the extreme. To quote from one study on hired killers, which applies to Sgt. Price, though not necessarily to all snipers: "They are surprisingly ordinary people without spectacular failings . . . (though) this kind of personality has difficulty forming lasting emotional relationships to people. The pendulum swings of emotion associated with some

64

psychoses are absent. (They) are rational in a negative and perverse Dostoyevskian sense and thoughtfully aware of their motives and the consequences of their acts. Feeling neither joy nor sadness and indifferent to death, they are unable to relate to others. (He) accurately perceives reality but is limited in his capacity to respond to it emotionally. To paraphrase G. K. Chesterton: He is not someone who has lost his reason, rather he is someone who has lost everything but his reason. . . ."

And there was something one of Price's commanders from Vietnam had said that stuck in Walter McGrane's mind, made him shiver down inside when he thought of it: "I knew Clayton Price from 'Nam and later on in Africa when I was doing some freelance work. Man, he was scary. I always was glad he was on our side in those days, though I'm not sure whose side he might be on now. Being up against Clayton Price is like shooting pool with Pool itself; give him the break and he'll run the table on you. Afterward, he'll read the morning paper and never look back."

Only four or five of the old ones were left now. But within the Covert Operations Unit, where Walter McGrane drew his pay, they were legends of a sort, discussed over coffee and after-dinner drinks at good restaurants.

"Christ, can you believe this: Morelock once hit a VC at twenty-five hundred yards with a fifty-caliber machine gun converted into a sniper weapon. Shot him right off a goddamned bicycle."

"I know Morelock holds the all-time kill record from 'Nam. Who's second?"

"Tortoise — Price — I think. If I recall correctly, he had eighty-two confirmed, something over two hundred more classified as 'probables.' "

The stories went on, the legends endured, about White Feather and Centipede and Tortoise and the rest. They were the colorful ones. White Feather had become an instructor at Quantico; the rest, those who weren't dead or retired, were still out there someplace, lying in wait until called upon by whatever or whoever required their services. And McGrane knew their credo, their simple and overriding criterion for success: one shot, one kill. In Vietnam, the average number of rounds expended per kill by ordinary soldiers was in the range of two hundred thousand to four hundred thousand. The snipers had averaged 1.3 per kill. At three for two, Price had fallen below the standard in Puerto Vallarta.

In his associations with the shadowmen, Walter McGrane had always been surprised at how ordinary they seemed, no spectacular failings that one might notice right off. But he'd read the psychological evaluations: "The subjects all possess great courage, a high tolerance for discomfort and for being alone for extended periods of time. However, they share a common trait of being unable to form lasting emotional relationships with other people. Though they perceive reality much more directly, quickly, and accurately than most, they are limited in their capacities to respond to it emotionally. For example, the exhaustive studies by Ingram and Marks have disclosed a remarkable lack of hate directed at the enemy. On the contrary, the so-called shadowmen seem to have only respect for the enemy and no thought of killing for revenge. According to Ingram and Marks, that latter characteristic is partly a tactic for completing the mission, partly a matter of survival. Maintaining an emotional distance from the quarry focuses concentration and prevents the man from making foolish mistakes based on personal reasons, which would render him both ineffective and vulnerable."

Walter McGrane looked out the window at black night roaring by. "Personal reasons" . . . Therein lay the fault and the flaw of what had once been a perfect killing machine. Clayton Price had made that mistake, reducing his emotional distance from a target. Had taken that distance down to zero, in fact, and got too close, even though he'd been warned years ago to forget his one personal vendetta.

Click, and click again — the sniper rifle. Walter McGrane looked at the man called Weatherford and the other muscled windbreaker beside Weatherford. They were the new and improved versions of Clayton Price, routinely produced by special operations units in various branches of the military. Better trained, disciplined, more reliable, it was said, unlike the shadowmen, who were viewed by some as too individualistic, too eccentric, too likely to just take off and do things their own way. "Cowboys," they were sometimes called, the word accompanied always by a derisive shake of the head. Still, others in the COU, Walter McGrane included, preferred the old way of working, using the shadowmen who left no paper trail of temporary assignments from the military, a set of specialized arrows that could be drawn from a quiverful of options when the time arose. The few who were left could be called on when the times got tough and the work got extremely dirty, "wet" in agency par-

lance, in Africa or the Middle East or Gua-
temala . . . or Mexico. True, they weren't
as disciplined as their newer versions. And,
true, they tended to be eccentric. But they
had their own strengths. Individualism and
eccentricity always seemed to be the other
side of the creative mind.

The Lear's engines shifted in pitch, and
the co-pilot announced over the intercom they
were beginning their descent into San Antonio
for refueling. Weatherford looked over at
Walter McGrane and grinned. "Just who is
it we're after, this time? All we were told
was to gather up our gear and get over to
Andrews."

"Man named Clayton Price."

"Don't believe I've heard of him. That
never matters, though, does it?"

"It might this time," said Walter McGrane.

"Why's that?"

"He's one of us. Going up against Clayton
Price is like shooting pool with Pool itself."

"What's that mean?"

"It means after you finish making love to
that rifle, you might want to glance at the
notes I prepared for you."

"Right, I'll do that."

"Yes," Walter McGrane said, "be sure and
do that. And remind me to tell you sometime
about what he went through in Vietnam, after

his capture by the VC."

"Bad?"

Walter McGrane looked Weatherford straight in the eyes and shook his head slowly back and forth, said nothing, and returned to studying his maps.

Gypsy Music

Twenty minutes after turning west off Route 200, Danny got lost in Zacualtán, feeling ugly and incompetent about it. Not much of a town, but the streets all seemed to end in fields or at somebody's front porch. He and Luz had driven this route once before on a weekend outing, and she remembered something about the plaza. Turn there, maybe. Danny drove back through town, made the turn, and three blocks later they were heading up the coast road, in open country again. The shooter was quiet, desert boot tapping slowly on the dashboard.

This was backcountry rural, where anything might be wandering on or across the road. Animals, in particular, liked to lie on the warm pavement when the night cool settled in and sometimes shared that space with drunks. Danny held the Bronco back, which wasn't hard since Vito complained and got out of sorts at anything exceeding fifty.

Around three A.M., the pavement ended at a barricade of hundred-pound rocks

71

painted white and marked with the words *"NO PASEO."*

Danny whacked the steering wheel. "Shit."

Nothing about a detour, nothing in the way of directions. When they'd come this way a couple of years back, there was no problem, pavement all the way. Rough, but passable then.

Luz rescued them for the second time in forty-five minutes. "Danny, bus going through village."

"Where?"

"Down hill, over there."

Danny looked down to his left and saw the lights of a bus moving at about three miles an hour, its headlights illuminating trees and houses. He retreated down the hill and took the Bronco into the village, figuring the busdriver knew something they didn't, something about a detour. Danny tried to guess where the bus had come through the narrow dirt streets winding into one another. He made a left turn at what he thought was a road and ended up in a creek bed, where the headlights startled roosting chickens and sleeping pigs. Finally he worked his way through the village, made the right choice at a Y intersection, and got back up on the main road. After a mile of fine dust blowing into the Bronco and covering everything inside with a kind of brownish red talcum powder, they passed two bulldozers sitting in the dark and hit hard surface again.

They were moving along the edge of a high cliff dropping off toward the Pacific and could see the lights of Santa Cruz, and San Blas farther on, a long way to the north. Dawn coming up on the other side of the coastal mountains. Danny estimated they were an hour out of San Blas and drove carefully around curve after curve, with jungle on both sides of them and trees arching over the road, making a gray green tunnel through which the mad trio rolled at sunrise, all with their own oblique purposes.

Luz was curled up in the back, sleeping, almost out of sight in the jumble of water jugs, food, and other gear. The daughter of Jesús and Esmeralda Santos could sleep anywhere at anytime in anything.

The shooter lit another Marlboro, stretched, yawned.

"What business you in, Mr. Schumann, if you don't mind my asking?" Country-boy language, casual approach. Danny watched the road for serious potholes but was aware the shooter was looking at him for several seconds before answering.

"Consulting. You could say I'm a freelance specialist in crisis management." Suitably vague, but the hair on the back of Danny's neck lifted up. He got hold of himself and pushed it a little further.

"Any special area in which you work? Construction, oil, any of that?"

"All of it. If there's a mess, I clean up the trash, get rid of the garbage. It's a dirty world, lot of messy accounts out there."

Danny was about to ask him what messy accounts had to be settled in Puerto Vallarta, just to see how he'd answer, but the shooter spoke first.

"How about you, Danny Pastor? What's your game?" He talked quietly, and it was hard to hear him over the roar of the wind from their passing. Danny had to lean toward him to catch all the words.

"Aw, I just hang around Puerto Vallarta. Saved up a little money a while back, and I'm living on that."

"You don't do anything, then? Just lie around Las Noches with the rest of the gringos? I stopped in there the other day. What a pile of dog crap that was — all of them flopped in beach chairs, stomachs bulging, drinking beer and telling lies. Looked to me like kind of a kamikaze lifestyle. Ever go there?"

A feeling kept coming back to Danny that what he was doing was the wrong thing to be doing, that he might be in over his head. "C'mon, Pastor," his brain was talking again, "hang together, he's just fishing. You're a smart guy, dominate him. You know the big secret about him. He doesn't know anything about you. Do the kind of work you're capable of doing."

"Yeah, I go to Las Noches sometimes."

"I had you pegged for a writer, something like that." The shooter let a few seconds go by, then added, "I always thought I'd like to put some things down on paper. You ever do any writing?"

Christ, this guy was unbelievable. Danny's confidence was lurching back in the direction of shaky. He'd started out thinking about the matchup between a robot assassin — cocky and crude like the wiseguys, but dumber, he figured — and a crack reporter, which shouldn't have been any contest at all. Yet Danny kept getting the sense of the shooter being something more than an eye and a gun.

Danny's old skills were latent, but back there someplace. He kept telling himself that. Still, the booze and sun and loose life in general had dulled him. He'd been aware of that happening but never noticed how far he'd dropped until that moment. He was feeling rusty and rattled but kept talking to himself: Get tough, get smart, get on top of him. So

75

what if you're a writer. That doesn't mean anything as long as he doesn't catch on to what you know.

"I did a little writing once. Nothing recently."

"Got a case of . . . what do they call it? . . . writer's block?"

"I never much liked that term. It's a copout way of looking at things, like some invisible force has a fist around your mind and is squeezing it."

"Well, then what would you call it?" Desert boot tapping on the dash, cigarette ashes flipped into the wind.

Danny listened to the hum of Vito's tires. He jerked the wheel and took the Bronco around a bad hole in the pavement, settled down again. Looked at his watch and couldn't see the dial in bad light.

"It's almost six," the shooter said. "I've always been fascinated with writers. So if it's not writer's block, what is it?"

Danny had started out to interview the shooter. But the shooter was curling things back around on him, doing a neat Socratic sideslip.

"Like I said before, calling it writer's block kind of lets you off the hook. When I'm writing and get stuck, I prefer to think of it as a conceptual problem I have to work out.

Intellectual gridlock you've got to get by."

"I like that." The shooter unscrewed the top of a water jug and took a long drink, replaced the top. "Puts the responsibility back on yourself rather than thinking some mysterious outside force is in control of your destiny."

"You don't believe in outside forces? In bad luck?"

"Not much. I suppose it happens. But a whole lot of people blame their predicaments on bad luck rather than taking responsibility for the situation they've gotten themselves into and for getting out of that situation and on to something better. You're about entitled to what you get and not too much more."

Danny tried to climb back on top of the dialogue. "You travel a lot in your line of work?"

"Quite a bit. How'd you end up in Puerto Vallarta? Not running from the IRS, I hope."

Damn, if this was some kind of Socratic game, the shooter was good. One of Danny's old professors in journalism school used to say, "Ask short questions, keep *them* talking, avoid the tendency to get into a lecture yourself."

"Got divorced a while back. Running from her and the memories, not the IRS. Looking for warmer weather. Just drifted down here.

Where do your travels take you?"

The shooter flipped his cigarette out, and Danny could see sparks in the rearview mirror where it hit the pavement. "Wherever there's something gunking up the system. Like I said, garbage cleanup. What do you think of those two guys back in Puerto Vallarta . . . Willie and Lobo? Like their music?"

"Yeah, how'd you know?" Danny looked over at him, looked quick, then stared at the road.

"Saw you and her in a place the other night." The shooter canted his head back toward where Luz was sleeping. "Seemed like you were having a good time, dancing around the tables and all that. What's that place called? Seafood soup, green salads . . ."

"You mean Mamma Mia?" Danny had a strange feeling that someone was swinging a big stick from behind him where he couldn't see it coming.

"That's it . . . Mamma Mia. I thought the music was pretty decent. Has a certain power, certain energy to it, don't you think? What kind of music would you call it? Never heard anything quite like it before."

"I don't know. Willie and Lobo call it 'gypsy-jazz' or something along those lines."

They were running hard down a long hill, coming into Santa Cruz, jungle giving way to fields. In spaces between the trees Danny could see breakers hitting the shore a few miles west of them. Farther out and beyond mountain shadow, the ocean was colored soft rose. A hundred miles south of them, Walter McGrane's Learjet was beginning its descent into Puerto Vallarta.

The shooter bent over, reached in a side pocket of his knapsack, and took out a fresh pack of Marlboros. "The world can never have too much gypsy music."

Danny thought about that and it seemed right, some elemental truth. Seemed like there was something in what the shooter had said that went beyond music. Something to do with firelight and fast guitars and the stamp of bare feet near painted wagons that would roll when morning came. Something to do with moving quick and living off your wits, like the shooter was doing, like Danny was trying to do.

The road curved west for a mile and took them down to the outskirts of Santa Cruz. Danny turned right and ran parallel to the Pacific, which was a block or so to their left, past cottages for rent and cottages for sale. Mexican tourists came here; so did a few gringos. In the mirror, Danny could see Luz sitting up.

He looked over at the shooter. "Think

maybe we ought to stop, get a little rest? I'm feeling sort of numb and scratchy."

"Sounds right to me. I'm tired myself. Know any place to stay?"

"Yeah, there's two or three places in San Blas, as I remember. One called Las Brisas is pretty nice. The others are a little rough, but okay."

"Let's try the better one." His choice made sense. Stay where the gringos were mostly likely to stay, be less noticeable that way.

Las Brisas had its doors open, but the desk was closed. Luz talked to an old man tending things, came back to the Bronco, and said there wouldn't be anyone there to check them in until eight o'clock, an hour and a half farther on. The shooter was watching uniformed navy personnel from the military installation in San Blas walk by the Bronco, on their way to defend the shores of Mexico. Somewhere back in the hotel grounds a parrot was jabbering.

"You said there's another place?" The shooter looked dying tired, the lines under his eyes fanning out into concentric semicircles.

"Yeah, a few blocks from here. The best part about it is the stuffed crocodile in the lobby and an old copy of the buccaneer's creed of freedom etched on the wall. San Blas has a colorful history, not to mention the worst bug problem of any place you'll ever be. The damn bugs can drive you crazy."

"Let's find some breakfast, then come back here and check in." He was still watching military people walking by.

At eight-fifteen they were back at Las Brisas. Still no desk clerk. Luz told the night boy, who was about eighty, that her gringo friends were getting tired and cranky. A few minutes later a woman in a nightdress and bathrobe appeared and checked them in. They'd gotten her up, and she wasn't happy about it. Danny took a room for Luz and him, another for the shooter.

They were a bad-looking outfit, wrinkled and beat, sweat coming heavy again in the humidity of the Mexican coast and streaking down through the dust in which they'd bathed at the road construction site. The woman behind the desk studied Luz's "Puerto Vallarta Squeeze" T-shirt, then glanced at the ceiling for a moment, thinking social changes were definitely needed but maybe not quite so much all at once.

Danny slept until a little after four in the afternoon. He woke up blinking, feeling grungy and groggy. Luz came out of the bathroom, naked, hair wet, and grinning at him. She had slightly oversize breasts for her general overall proportions and carried them high. They pulled up even higher when she reached behind her neck with both hands and twisted her hair. Along with good ol' Missy Morganthal back in his undergraduate days, who'd have shucked her jeans in the student union if he'd asked, Luz could get Danny up and rolling faster than any woman he'd ever known. But in that moment of waking and blinking and giving out dusty coughs, he needed coffee and a shower more than he needed Luz. Before he could even mention it, Luz stepped into underthings and said she'd run down coffee while Danny showered.

When he came out of the bathroom, the coffee was there and Luz was gone. He got dressed and stood outside the room, steaming cup in his right hand and a lazy sun headed toward evening. Luz was thirty yards away, sitting by the swimming pool, talking to someone in the water. Danny walked over.

The shooter was paddling around, doing a capable breast stroke. He pulled himself up and sat on the edge of the pool, looking good in his red-and-blue boxer trunks, looking in the body like he wasn't as old as his face indicated last night. Maybe six three, and lean, but strong in the shoulders and still having a pretty good chest and no belly at all. His knapsack was sitting near the edge of the pool where he could keep an eye on it.

"Buenas tardes," said the shooter, pushing back his wet hair until it lay straight and flat against his head.

That's when Danny noticed the scars on his legs, running all the way up his thighs and disappearing under the swimsuit. Mean, ugly scars, as if they'd come from a dirty knife and had never healed properly. More scars on his back and chest.

Danny recovered and said good afternoon back to him, then found a chair in the shade and brushed away no-see-ums that returned only a moment later, starting to sweat again in high coastal humidity.

The water had some appeal, but Danny hadn't brought a swimsuit. Neither had Luz, but she'd rolled up her jeans and was sitting on the edge of the pool, swishing her feet back and forth in the water. For some reason, she was smiling.

The shooter stood up, getting ready to go back to his room, knapsack dangling in his hand. "How about staying here for the night. Get rested, make good time tomorrow."

Danny said that was fine with him. Mexican highways at night were just too much work.

"You've been here before?" The shooter was running a towel over his hair.

"Yeah, once . . . in San Blas, that is. Several years ago, when I was drifting south. Stayed at the place with the stuffed crocodile and fought off bugs all night. The screens had holes in them."

Danny hadn't met Luz at that time and had spent an evening in an upstairs gringo bar, a place called Tacky Chuck's, looking out the window. Some kind of celebration had been going on, people marching around the plaza, a band playing. He'd talked with a young American woman named Stacie — 50 percent of young American women seemed to have that Christian name — who came from L.A. and whose conversation mostly consisted of "like . . . uh . . . you know." She told him she didn't believe . . . like, uh, you know . . . in institutionalized religion, that she worshiped God in her own way.

She'd asked Danny what he thought about the whole religion-God deal. He'd told her she was about as deep as sweat, philosophically, and paid his bar bill. He knew she'd eventually get hustled by some handsome Mexican waiter who'd tell her if he just had a little money, he'd be able to buy a motorboat and make a good living as a fisherman. After he got his boat, he'd beat her around until she took her fouled-up life down the road. It happened all the time.

But they kept coming down for more, the blondes and redheads and all other colors, divorced or on spring break or bought off by their parents to get the hell out of everybody's life and smoke their dope or take their troubles elsewhere. A fair number of them came to San Blas. Something to do with pirates, Danny figured, and some strange kind of female yearning for abuse, too. He'd once sat at a beach restaurant south of Puerto Vallarta with a woman who pointed out to the little cove nearby and said, "See all those boats bobbing out there? I think I bought every goddamned one of 'em." She'd been good-looking at one time, but the effects of sustained boat buying for fishermen who formerly had been waiters were showing on her. She'd been broke, and he'd treated her to a fancy tourist drink, for which she'd eventually been more than appreciative.

The shooter was cleaned up and walking across the Las Brisas courtyard toward Danny and Luz. His jeans and a khaki shirt both were holding a decent press in spite of the evening heat and humidity. The guy knew how to pack, that much was clear.

They drank in a little restaurant bar attached to the hotel, overhead fans pushing the same warm, damp air around and over them. Since the shooter was buying, Luz drank margaritas, sitting there in her jeans and sandals, white off-the-shoulder blouse. Danny ordered a beer and nursed it, working on staying reasonably alert.

The shooter took out his Marlboros, offered the pack to both Luz and Danny. Luz said no thank you, and Danny took one, saying, "I stopped smoking two years ago, then started again and quit and started. Now I'm quitting, but bumming." Mumbling, mumbling crap, said Danny to himself, and telling his mind to get steady.

After the shooter had lit his own cigarette, he slid the silver lighter toward Danny.

Danny lit his and handed the Zippo back to the shooter. "How long you been in Mexico?"

"Few days. Like I said last night, friend dropped me off his sailboat. Got our signals mixed, and he didn't come back for me."

Danny had noticed earlier the heavy bracelet on the shooter's right wrist but could see it better now. It had a large, deep-blue stone embedded in the silver, and Danny asked if he could take a closer look. The shooter took off the bracelet and handed it to him. Danny was surprised at its weight and said as much.

The shooter put it back on his wrist and shrugged. "Lots of silver in it, I guess. Bought it in the Middle East."

"When you came in by boat the way you did, how'd you check in with immigration?"

"I didn't. Didn't feel like bothering them." The shooter tilted up his Pacífico, Adam's apple working as the beer went down.

"You don't have a tourist card, then?" Danny already knew why. No tracks, no evidence he'd been in Mexico. Still, why risk being picked up for something like that, when he could have cooked up false papers? Unless he'd had to come in fast and didn't have time for paper shuffling.

The shooter smiled. "No tourist card; only figured on being there a day or two."

Luz was staring at the shooter in wonderment and wide in the eyes, looking over at Danny between stares. Danny wasn't surprised she was surprised. Here was a guy who didn't like airplanes or traveler's checks or credit cards or, for God's sake, tourist documents handed out routinely and generally without question. On the other hand, the odds of having your papers checked in a tourist town were just about zero unless you did something really stupid. If Luz had known what Danny knew, it would all make sense, but she didn't.

Danny pushed it, wanted to see what his plans were. "How the hell are you going to

87

get across the border? That's the first thing they want to see, especially at an out-of-the-way place like Sonoyta or whatever it's called."

"I'll work it out. Turn myself into a stone, have you catapult me over, something like that."

Danny thought, Now he's getting occult on me, runelike. The shooter was grinning, in kind of a viperish way, it seemed to Danny, while he ordered another Pacífico. Luz was still looking, first at the shooter, then at Danny, wondering about the ways of gringo men she'd known and marveling for about the zillionth time at their total concentration on being self-destructive.

The shooter added a postscript. "Don't worry about it; I'll figure something out. It's not your problem. Just get me within walking distance of the border and we'll consider it done. I understand *mordida*" — the bite — "works pretty well, a few bucks in a border official's hand, that sort of thing. If that fails, you can take me to one of the major crossing points and I'll slide through at rush hour."

He was right. That'd probably work, unless the border cops were looking for someone in particular, someone trying to get back to the United States fast.

Danny and the shooter ordered the fish special for dinner. Luz went for broiled shrimp in garlic butter. The sound system was playing American Dixieland jazz, out of keeping with the surroundings and some frail and failed attempt at pleasing gringos, making them feel like they weren't really too far from home. Danny listened to a nice trumpet solo on "Summertime" and ate his fish and brown rice, glancing up now and then at the shooter, who was asking Luz about her life. She was obviously pleased he'd asked.

She told him what Danny already knew, leaving out certain and significant parts, of course, and finished up by saying, "Danny came in the restaurant where I was working, one night. I liked him right away; he was more polite than most of the men. I remember he was going to order enchiladas, but I told him the chiles rellenos were better, that we had big chiles and big chiles are very good." She smiled at Danny, but the shooter didn't seem to be picking up on it, that chiles play a central role in Mexican sexual humor. To be a man and have a big chili is considered a good thing. Danny rolled his eyes and looked out the window.

The Dixieland band moved into "Muskrat Ramble." From the small aviary in the hotel courtyard, parrots took up where the trom-

bone left off: shufflin' . . . shufflin' . . .
arrrk!

Mosquitoes whined on the other side of the screen next to Danny, looking in at his face and neck: "Psst! Hey, you . . . gringo guy . . . come outside for just a little while, gringo." One of the cooks was laughing somewhere back in the kitchen, and the overhead fan turned slowly, reminding Danny of a boozy old song they used to sing about one of the early hangouts in Puerto Vallarta:

Layin' around the Oceana,
Overhead fans and no hot water.
Drinkin' tequila and teasing the girls,
Hustlin' a fisherman's daughter.

Luz was telling the shooter how much she wanted to live in the United States someday. He listened attentively, nodding from time to time, but didn't say anything.

The light was fading fast, almost gone.

Flamenco Afternoons

Four horses and a colt slumbered along Juárez, taking their time. Danny Pastor waited for them to move over, shifted up through the gears, and headed toward the outskirts of San Blas. There he turned east on a road that would take them up to Route 15, the main north-south highway in western Mexico. It was a good morning, mist coming off ponds and rivers and colored amberish by early light. A good morning, a full, bright morning in May, soft and warm and making it seem as if everything might turn out all right.

Still, Danny was impatient and the opposite of that, all at the same time, flopping around somewhere in the middle ambiguities. In his thoughtful moments he considered what would happen if they were stopped by one or another police outfit, trying to think what he might say about a passenger who carried no tourist card. Ordinarily that could be worked out with *mordida,* but it was hard to say what level of interest in gringos of all kinds had been generated by the killings in Puerto Vallarta. Maybe none at all, maybe a lot, maybe it was just being treated as a local problem. The conservative Danny was inclined to head for the border, fast. The other Danny knew he should take his time, get to know the shooter inside out, needed to do that if the story was going to be all it could be.

The shooter had put on dark green sunglasses and his ball cap, drinking coffee from a paper cup. He was wearing the same clothes as the night before, still reasonably pressed, in spite of the heat and humidity. His eyes were better this morning, not as tired. Danny, wearing green cotton shorts and an old, multiwrinkled ecru shirt with a plain collar, felt rumpled and disorderly compared with the shooter, who had an air of military about him, of neatness and slow, deliberate precision.

Luz was rested and showed it, smiling, bouncing along in her little space behind the shooter and Danny. She pointed at a long-tailed blue magpie jay flying through the trees to their right, morning light showing for an instant through the translucent blue of the bird's tail and wings. What could be better for her? Nothing. A pleasant morning and headed for *el Norte,* where she'd always wanted to go.

Two bobwhite quail scurried across the highway, running on short, quick legs, then lifted off and flickered into the Guaycoyul palms. Red-flowered trees, yellow-flowered trees. The shooter asked Luz about the red ones, and she replied, "*Tabachín,* Mexican bird of paradise."

They climbed east over the low coastal mountains and could see the Sierra Madre rising up fifty miles ahead of them, across a big valley, and the peaks looking light purple in the haze. Curves and hills, villages waking up, donkey carts and men on horseback driving cattle, schoolchildren walking along the road. Close-up smoke from cooking fires, distant smoke from slash-and-burn farming where hillsides were being cleared. Man along the highway with the two items most common to men walking along rural highways in Mexico: old brown dog and a machete. It was at least eighty and climbing fast. Danny was guessing at something over a hundred later on. Soft morning, flamenco afternoon.

The Bronco called Vito rolled north through an invisible communications web becoming more intricately dense by the hour, a humming meshwork of unseen words and orders reaching out with the single purpose of finding a man known as Tortoise. After

93

refueling in San Antonio, the Learjet out of Andrews had landed in Puerto Vallarta twenty-four hours ago. As instructed by the tower, the plane had been parked near a row of Mexican military aircraft at the edge of the airport. Walter McGrane and his compadres were picked up by a white Dodge van and taken away without passing through immigration or customs. Two hours later, heavily armed men had begun spreading out from various posts in Mexico, covering airports and bus terminals and railroad stations, riding through the countryside in trucks and vans. All of them on the watch for a man who'd cut down two people in Puerto Vallarta. And all of them had the same instructions: If Clayton Price was spotted, report in, but *do not engage*. Repeat: *Do not engage*.

Walter McGrane sat near the roar of a window air conditioner in the Puerto Vallarta police station, drinking coffee and trying to guess which way Clayton Price was headed. Weatherford and the other man were in the next room, speaking Spanish to each other, monitoring reports from the field. Nothing, so far. But something would turn up. It always did. And when it did, they would find Clayton Price and kill him and go home.

★ ★ ★

The shooter hadn't said anything since they'd left the Las Brisas, as if he were thinking hard and deep, though twice he'd turned to glance at Luz. At a little past nine they hit Route 15. Danny turned left with America-the-beautiful three days north of them. A Pemex station came up, and Danny filled both the front and rear tanks of the Bronco, put in a quart of oil. The attendant had tried the old gas-pump trick, neglecting to ratchet the dial back to zero before he stuck the nozzle in the Bronco. Danny'd caught him at it, put his hand on the attendant's arm, and pointed at the gauge. The attendant had merely shrugged, as if he'd forgotten that nicety in the process of providing good, fast service.

Little villages rolled by, some of them near the road, some a half mile or so on either side, hot and dirty and rough as hell. Ragged wash on clotheslines, brown dogs asleep in the shade, burros wandering around.

"Damn, that's tough living," Danny said, trying to make conversation. "Those places are pits."

The shooter looked and said nothing. He'd seen dusty little villages all over the world and had squatted in them and had eaten with his right hand when the villagers had some-

95

thing to spare. He'd always paid for what he'd eaten, unless it was the village custom to make travelers comfortable and where payment would be an insult. He'd eaten monkey and snake and bird and dog and croc and things in brown stew that floated greasy and fat, wondering if the greasy fat things also wondered about what their happy life had come to. Stew had a way of abolishing identity, mercifully so.

Passing by Santa Penita, an especially bad-looking potpourri of houses and dirt streets, Danny shook his head, glad he wasn't living there in heat and dust. No matter where he was headed, it would never come to that.

"I grew up in a village just like that one, lived in a house just like those, went to a little adobe school like the one we just went by." Luz was kneeling between them, looking out the windshield. "Danny, it's unkind to say and think such things. These are poor people; life is very hard for them."

She'd heard it before — gringo superiority, tourists openmouthed and aghast at how the po' folks live and why doesn't somebody do something about it, and what happens to all that foreign aid we send? That sort of bullshit clucking.

Danny turned to her. "You're right. Sorry."

The shooter was thinking along the same lines. "Doesn't make a whole lot of sense, you know. Americans born into luxury's cradle, then escaping it by running down here looking for meaning because all the crap we buy somehow doesn't cut it for us. And while we're looking, we're bitching about the sanitation setup of a destitute Mexican village. Ever strike you we're nuttier than hell, Danny Pastor?"

"Yeah, I know what you mean. Along with that, I remember the writer Carlos Fuentes saying all gringos look alike to Mexicans and our language sounds like Chinese to them."

The talk about place had given Danny an opening. "Where you from, originally?" He pretended to concentrate on driving, giving the impression he wasn't all that interested.

"Brooklyn, Seventh Avenue. Area called Park Slope."

"You grow up there?" Danny had a deep-down sense the quiet man was in a mood to talk.

"Partly. My father pulled out when I was ten." The shooter looked over at him, a kind of dark rain moving across his face.

He was calling up old images, bad things that happened. His voice took on that color and sounded distant, maybe lonely, maybe all of that and something more. For a moment

Danny thought the conversation was over, but the shooter went on. "Don't know why he left. Never did understand it. Just left. My mother couldn't take care of both of us, so she sent me off to live with her mother and father in northern Minnesota. The ol' man drank a lot. My grandmother was pretty nice, but they were in their seventies by that time. Not ready to take up being parents again."

Danny was surprised at what the shooter was saying, talking personal stuff, perfect background information and context for the events of two nights ago. "Minnesota sounds pretty good. I went through there once. Lots of water, clean."

"It's all right. When the ol' man was off the bottle he taught me to hunt and fish. Did a lot of that. All of 'em are dead now, my mother included."

Danny bored in. "Ever see your father again . . . after he left?"

"Once. He and my mother got back together again and came down to Parris Island when I finished boot camp. Didn't have much to say to them. . . ."

The shooter let it go, his voice circling down. He lit a cigarette and watched the dry, flat countryside rolling by, the Sierra Madre tracking along parallel to them forty miles east. A little farther on Luz said something Danny couldn't make out over the wind blasting through the Bronco and the roar of a low-geared engine.

The shooter heard her. "She wants to visit the cemetery where her parents are buried. Says it's down toward someplace called Teacapán."

"Ceylaya." Luz was nearly shouting, trying to make Danny hear. "My parents are buried there. I have not visited their graves in four years."

"Luz, this isn't any goddamned tour. It's a long way to the border. Maybe we'll stop on the way back if it works out and you can visit all the cemeteries you want." Danny was saying those things, knowing he wouldn't do it, knowing he'd make up another excuse on the way back. Sometimes you say those things anyway.

Silver-and-green Pacífico buses, big trucks, long line of them jammed up on a hill, bathing Vito in black exhaust fumes. Then over the Río San Pedro bridge, where a huge chunk was missing from the cement railing on the right. Danny had seen those gaps all over Mexico and always wondered for a moment who and what went over the side and never came back and how long it'd been since they'd done it.

The shooter was looking at the road map while Danny looked over his shoulder at Luz. She was near to crying, her eyes looking wet and infinitely black in the way they got when she was sad. Danny felt like a real shithead, but there was work to be done. A delivery job, information gathering, lot of work. Besides, he'd never liked cemeteries of any kind. Luz sat in the jumble where she rode, staring west out a side window of the Bronco.

The shooter folded the map. "If you take a little road out of Escuinapa and run west toward the sea, you go right past Ceylaya." He unbuttoned his right shirt pocket and took out three hundred dollars American, handed it to Danny. "Let her visit the cemetery, what the hell . . . hour down to the coast, hour back. We'll find someplace on the beach for lunch. All right?"

Luz was listening, watching them.

Danny felt like crap. Take the money and he'd be showing love for lucre but not really caring at all about Luz or her family's graves. Don't take it and he'd piss off both her and the shooter. The shooter had put Danny in a hard place, and he didn't like it, made him a little scarlet in the face.

Danny turned half around and said, "We'll go down to Ceylaya, Luz. Stop crying, for chrissake."

He gave the money back to the shooter. "Here, it's your trip. The money we agreed on is enough." Greed had its limits. Not often, but sometimes.

In Escuinapa the shooter watched a señorita cross the street in front of them while they were stopped for a light. She was taller than most Mexican women and longer in the legs, in tight cutoff jeans and a peach top similar to a man's sleeveless undershirt. Under the cloth her breasts swung pleasantly back and forth as she walked. Good-looking woman, long brown hair with copper highlights and almost Asian in her facial structure. She carried a plate of food, and the shooter watched her until she turned in a storefront.

He looked over at Danny and grinned, little embarrassed kind of grin coming from the fact Danny had seen him watching the woman. He shook his head a bit, as if to say "Real nice."

Or maybe "It's been a long time."

Or maybe "Wish I was younger."

As they moved along the street, the shooter turned and stared at the doorway where the señorita had disappeared. In the store window were steel tips for spear guns, ends for outboard motor gas lines, two mouthpieces for trumpets, camera, film, masks for scuba diving, handheld telephones, car and boat oil,

101

flares, blank audiotapes, two flatirons, basketball, two soccer balls, compasses, padlocks, fishing lures, swimming goggles, car headlights, clocks.

Danny turned west toward the sea while Luz was watching the shooter, who had watched the young woman in a peach top.

Six miles down the road they crossed a long bridge across some kind of backwater. A village sat on the far side of the water, off to the right. In front of the third house along a dirt street was a cage under a banana tree, and whatever was in the cage prowled back and forth.

The shooter saw it, too, pointing. "What's that all about? The cage?"

"I don't know. Mexicans keep all kinds of animals for pets."

"Pull over. I'd like to see whatever it is up close."

To Danny, this *was* starting to feel like a tour. But what the hell. He swung into the village and drove up the dirt street, stopping in front of the third house.

In the cage, brown spots on buff gray fur moved behind heavy wire. An ocelot, full grown, was pacing rapidly in a space only a little longer than its own body, barely room enough for it to turn around. And it was two short steps to one end, where it wheeled and took two steps back to where it had started in some kind of mindless protest, the sequence repeating over and over in an eternal journey taking it nowhere.

Danny's stomach turned just watching it; he could sense, feel, its desperation, a kind of impotent fury or raging agony or whatever feelings humans ascribe to animal behavior. Years before, he'd interviewed a zoologist who was on one of her tours talking about chimpanzees. In preparation for the interview, he'd done some reading on animal behavior and found that animals in captivity undergo change, were not the same animals they started out to be. It was bad enough in zoos, but in close quarters such as the ocelot's cage, they went the human equivalent of insane. Danny mentioned that, and the three of them sat there for a minute looking at an ocelot no longer an ocelot, but something else, some creature existing nowhere else except in this village, in this yard, in this cage under a banana tree.

"How much you think they'd sell it for?" The shooter's eyes never left the animal.

"The cat? You thinking of buying it?"

"Yes."

"Then what?"

"We'll let it go. They're almost extinct in this part of Mexico, all over, I guess. Read that in a magazine a while back."

Jesus-on-the-dashboard, talk about nutty stuff, talk about crazy. Danny could see it all: him driving, Luz sitting on an assassin's lap, while three inches behind the driver was an insane ocelot, and all of them heading toward a cemetery Danny didn't want to visit in the first place.

Still, he understood the shooter's point. "Probably want thousands of dollars for it. Five, ten thousand, I really don't know. Not only do zoos love 'em, but fancy ladies covet ocelot coats."

"I don't have that much extra money with me. How long does it take to get money down here by wire?"

"Hard to say. Two days, a week, maybe, for the kind of money you're talking about. Start transferring that much and everybody gets interested, including the DEA in the United States. They all figure you're dealing dope."

The shooter lay back in his seat, face clenched and hard. "Let's roll."

"It's a tough world," Danny said, shifting gears, getting back up on the pavement. "Ever been to a bullfight? That's something else all over again, a ceremony about death, about the control of man over an animal."

"No. I refuse to go." The shooter was still

looking straight ahead, lips almost closed while he talked. "But it gets worse than bull-fights. Ever hear of the sanguinary *fiestas populares?* Translates as 'bloody festivals.' Have them in Spain all the time. I saw one once. Couldn't believe it."

"Can't say I have."

"There're different versions of it, depending on the place and the fiesta in progress. One version, one they like in Coria, is where a bull is set free in a street. People try to put out its eyes with steel-tipped darts, the literal version of a bull's-eye. Clever, huh? After a while the bull is full of darts, stuck in him every which way and all over and staggering around.

"Then the crowd starts torturing him, beating on him and pulling his tail and stabbing him with metal spikes that have barbs on them. Finally the bull is killed and castrated. When that's done, the fun seekers — and we're talking men, women, *and* children — smear themselves with its blood. The climax is parading the poor sonuvabitch's testicles around town as part of the celebration. Other versions involve dwarves or clowns mocking the real bullfights by using calves. It's torture, pure and simple. I like most Spanish and Mexican people I meet, but I've never understood the way some of them treat animals, particularly when all of that shit is done under the heading of religion, which it often is. Hell, in Spain even the local priests come out to bless the affair. Maybe they do here, for all I know."

"Well, we hang 'em up and slit their throats in packing houses," Danny said. "Hunt 'em down with high-power rifles. See any difference?"

"I see a big difference, but I don't much like that, either. Hunted animals when I was a kid, don't anymore. Got this notion of parallel civilizations in my head. Has to do with the equality of living things . . . all things . . . rocks and trees and ocelots and bulls and humans, learning to love the snake as much as you love the butterfly. Not sure when I started thinking like that."

He paused, looking out the side window. "Ah, to hell with it all."

Danny felt like mentioning the dogfights and cockfights and animal mutilations that still went on in the States, but he could see the shooter was in a nasty mood and left him alone with his contradictions.

On the edge of Ceylaya, the shooter and Danny sat in the Bronco while Luz walked up a long hill to the cemetery. Flies everywhere and hot wind and a young boy driving a herd of cattle past them along the road.

106

They swatted flies while the shooter watched Luz through the heat waves. After a while, saying nothing, he got out and followed her. In central Mexico's hottest time of the year, the sun was a laser and beat upon him as he climbed the hill. Danny watched him tug a bandanna from his right hip pocket, wiping his face and neck while he walked.

Luz was kneeling in the middle of the little graveyard. The shooter walked over to her and stood quietly, noticing how her hair clung to the back of her neck and how her brown skin shone from sweat and sunlight. After a minute or two, she rose, and Danny could see her saying something to him. The shooter nodded and they talked, at first not smiling, then smiling a little as they came slowly down toward the Bronco.

When they were twenty yards out, Luz stopped and gathered a handful of flowers, asking the shooter to hold them while she got settled in Vito. He looked slightly uncomfortable clutching flowers, and when he handed them back to Luz, one fell from his hands and blew into the ditch on a gust of morning wind. Luz said never mind, but he retrieved the single yellow flower and held it out to her. As Danny started the engine and headed toward the beach, Luz was bending toward the flowers and smelling them.

107

The shooter watched the road ahead, and smiled.

By the number of Tecate bottles on the table in front of them, Danny guessed the hombres in the Teacapán beach restaurant had been drinking beer for a couple of hours, since late morning, maybe. The men had pulled a Dodge pickup close to where they were sitting and had the doors swung open with the truck radio pounding like the heat itself. The hood on the truck was raised, and one of them had apparently been working on it, judging by the oil and grease on his light cotton shirt. Danny could smell gasoline and concluded that he'd been fiddling with the carburetor.

There were eight of them, drinking and sweating under the thatched roof, laughing too loudly for whatever the occasion might be, fingering their machetes lying on the table. One of them set a beer bottle on the blade of his machete and flipped the bottle end over end into the air, trying to catch it on the blade when it fell. The reach of his intent far exceeded his skill, and the bottle broke on the tabletop. His compadres laughed.

Luz whispered the Mexican word for drunks — *"borrachos."*

The juggler looked over at Danny, Luz, and the shooter, mean little sneer on his face. The song blasting from the truck radio had something to do with *norteamericanos*, something about what rich, sloppy jerks they were and how poorly they treated the migrant laborers stooped low in the fields of their truck farms. Danny picked up that much.

Within two minutes, all eight were looking at Danny, Luz, and the shooter, talking in the way drunken men all over the world talk. Get two or more of them together — Mexican or otherwise — get them drinking a little, and the testosterone seems to obtain a multiplier effect from alcohol and numbers. Here in a thatched roof bar on the coast of Mexico, an extra dimension of the thing called machismo was sprinkled over the hormones and mob bravado.

It was the kind of situation where you think, God, I'm glad I don't have a woman with me, especially a pretty one. But Danny did, and she was Mexican and she was with two gringos, and that just complicated things even more. Danny was watching the shooter's face and could tell he didn't like what was going on, either. But he was staying quiet, drinking his beer, keeping one foot against his knapsack under the table.

"Hey, gringo, got a match?" Oily Shirt was

leaning backward toward the shooter, speaking rough English. The shooter looked at him for a long moment, then reached in his left breast pocket and took out the silver lighter.

"Oh, no, amigo." The *borracho* laughed and switched over to Spanish, black hair falling partly over his face. "I no longer need a match, I have found it — my butt and your face."

Evidently the shooter didn't understand, since he continued to hold the lighter toward the Mexican. The entire table of them was roaring with smart-ass laughter now. They'd found someone to ridicule, someone so old and afraid, he'd still light their cigarettes even after they'd insulted him.

One of them shouted, *"Pollo,"* clucking and squawking in a bad imitation of a barnyard hen, at the same time holding up his right hand with only the first and little fingers extended — "Screw you" in Mexican sign language — and burbled through his laughter, *"No huevos"* — literally, "no eggs," "no balls." It was a way of showing the pretty señorita what cowards gringos really were. Danny started to make getting-up-and-leaving moves.

Oily Shirt decided to let the shooter light a cigarette, since the thin, gray-haired man in jeans and khaki shirt and ball cap was

110

clearly anxious to please and thereby avoid any trouble. The man shook out a cigarette and leaned toward the shooter.

What happened next happened fast, and Danny wasn't quite sure how it got done, but the shooter torched the Mexican's oil- and grease- and gasoline-soaked shirt with his lighter. The man jumped around, slapping at the flames and trying to unbutton the shirt all at the same time, couldn't get it off in his panic, and began running for the ocean twenty yards away. Danny knew the three of them were in real trouble and already had Luz on her feet and heading toward the Bronco.

One of the other hombres grabbed a machete and came toward the shooter, swinging it. The shooter went into a half crouch, executed some kind of martial arts move — graceful-like, arms and long thin legs all moving at the same time — and the Mexican went to his knees, nose smashed and bent sideways, piece of broken cheekbone poking through his skin, machete lying in the sand beside him. Two others jumped up. The shooter reached under his shirt in the back and pulled out a knife with a bone handle and four-inch blade. Everything stopped for a moment, while the bar owner screamed at all of them.

After a few seconds, the shooter picked up his knapsack and walked toward the Bronco, looking over his shoulder once. The hombres stayed where they were, stunned by what had happened. The man with the burned shirt and burned chest came out of the water, stumbling across the sand toward the Bronco, tatters of shirt waving and arms flailing, calling the shooter everything bad you can say in colloquial Mexican Spanish when you're mad and ready to kill. The shooter let him come on, then kicked him in the crotch when he got close enough.

Danny started Vito. The shooter slid in and looked down at the Mexican puking on the beach.

"Let's get out of this shithole," he said, sticking the knife back under his shirt.

He lit a cigarette and settled back in his seat, watching the hombres as the Bronco went past them. He wasn't smiling, yet he didn't look particularly mad, either. Danny was shaking and checked his side mirror, where he could see two of the hombres gathered around their fallen amigo on the beach. The man was still on his hands and knees, retching. Under the thatched roof, the others were tending to the man whose nose had been smashed and whose face would never look the same.

A few miles down the road, Danny calmed a little and glanced over at the shooter, noticing a bad scrape on the left side of his face, just in front of his ear. He'd poured some water on a blue bandanna and was dabbing at the scrape.

"You okay?" Danny asked, feeling bad about not helping him out in the fight, though not too bad, since he wouldn't have been much help.

The shooter didn't look at Danny, but continued working on his face with water and cloth. "Yeah, edge of the machete just clipped me when it came out of his hand. It was a stupid thing to do. I'm getting too old for that nonsense, letting pride overcome good judgment. I know better and should've just backed out of it."

He was missing part of the cut as he worked on it. Luz reached out and took the bandanna from him, steadied his neck with her right hand, and gently wiped away blood with her other hand. He stiffened a little, either because of the touch of her hand on his neck or because of the wound. Danny couldn't tell which. After that, the man who called himself Peter Schumann sat very still while she cleaned up his face.

"You sure seemed to handle it all right."

The shooter dug around in his knapsack,

brought out a tube of ointment, and smeared it on the cut. "It was stupid. There were eight of them. If they'd all come at once, we'd still be back there, and I'd have a lot more to tend to than a minor scrape. There's been a general decline in the gene pool all over, and it's best just to ignore it. You can't fight the world."

"I feel bad about not helping you out."

"No, you did the right thing, getting Luz out of there. You'd have just been in my way. I'm used to taking care of myself."

"Where'd you learn to fight like that? Was it karate or what?" What Danny was really wondering was how far things would have had to go before he'd have used the gun in the knapsack.

He wasn't smiling. "Combination of things I picked up a long time ago." He sighed, leaned back, and lit another cigarette, watching the countryside going by.

A minute or two passed, then he said, "Wonder what it feels like to be an insane ocelot . . . inside the head, you know. Must be colored a burning red orange . . . what you'd see in there, like fire so hot you can't stand it, like a white-hot poker on the tongue . . . like fire ants crawling around in your rectum."

He was talking to himself more than to

Danny. Danny let it go by and glanced over his shoulder at Luz. She sat quietly, looking at the back of the shooter's head. After a while she came to her knees and put her chin on Danny's shoulder, put a hand inside his shirt. The wound on the shooter's face looked dry-blood red and sore. Luz took her hand out of Danny's shirt and laid it on the shooter's arm. The shooter didn't move and kept staring straight ahead.

When they passed Ceylaya again, Luz turned and sat looking through the rear window of Vito. The village lay a quarter mile off the road.

She had been born there, María de la Luz Santos, born low. How far down? Being the last of six children in a Mexican peasant family, and a girl to boot, was bad enough. Because the other five were all boys, she'd started out twenty-some cuts beneath rock bottom. The social rankings worked to favor gender first, age after that. The males dominated, and deference to them was compulsory, particularly and especially to the father. Tack youth on to that, and María de la Luz Santos had been subservient to everyone.

Such was the order of things. Hard, but double hard when you had the kind of dreams Luz had, even as a young girl. Hazy dreams from the old magazines she'd read, from the embellished stories migrants had told when they'd returned from *el Norte*. Even without that information Luz would have had her own dreams; she was that way.

She'd awakened before dawn in late summer of 1983, eight years before she would meet Danny. Roosters crowing, first light coming, mist over the fields, and a feathery breeze through the village called Ceylaya. She'd helped her mother cook breakfast for her father and brothers. Before seven o'clock, Jesús Santos and his three eldest sons had pedaled rickety bicycles to the chili plantation where they worked eleven hours for low wages. The two younger boys spent the day working in the family's portion of the communal fields.

On that morning ten years ago, her stomach had hurt and she'd bled a little the day before. She was twelve, and something was happening inside her body she didn't understand, since her mother had never told her about menstrual cycles or anything else connected with womanhood. But the bleeding scared Luz, so when pressed, and looking at the young black eyes asking questions, her mother tried to explain as best she could. She'd said this was God's way of preparing Luz to have a family.

Luz had also asked if she might have a

blanket of her own. It hadn't seemed right anymore to be sharing one with the youngest boy, Pedro, and sleeping on the straw floor mat next to him, since he was now fifteen and once or twice his morning erection had accidentally touched her while he slept. She'd been too embarrassed to speak of these things, but clearly it was time for a blanket of her own. Her mother had said she would talk to Luz's father about it.

The roosters were joined by other village sounds, and Luz, twelve years old and dreaming, had thought of the day to come. She would sweep the dirt floors of the two-room house, sew, and pat-pat tortillas in a rhythm her mother called the heartbeat of Mexico. It was too dark to see what hung on the adobe walls, but she'd known what hung there from having looked at those walls for all the years of her life: old newspapers and calendars, a few religious posters, and one photograph of Jesús and Esmeralda Santos on their wedding day. The photograph, yellowing and curled a little, would have been nicer if a drunken hombre hadn't been holding a glass and looking over her parents' shoulders when the picture was taken.

In the front room her other four brothers had been waking up. The boys shared two beds, and between the beds was a wooden table holding a stack of schoolbooks and Catholic religious pamphlets. Below the table was a wooden chest where the family records were kept, baptismal and birth certificates, and a few more photos taken on special occasions, such as Jesús-the-second's confirmation day. Esmeralda Santos was allowed a corner of the chest for her single pair of shoes and the one good dress she owned.

In the afternoon Luz had helped the younger boys in the fields, bending low, picking vegetables her mother sold to other villagers. Out there in the sun, Luz's feed-sack dress had blown up around her legs and her straw hat flapped in the wind and dust, but the string around her chin held the hat close to her thick black hair.

Coming home from the fields in those times, Luz had kept her eyes straight ahead, not looking at the men in the outdoor cantina who already were watching her as she passed. It was understood she would marry one of the younger ones and keep his house and bear his children. "As many children as God decides," was the church's rule, though the village women seemed unconvinced when they said it. In the way things were, and are, Luz would be expected to endure her husband's beatings when he'd turn up drunk and to treat him perpetually as if he were his own small god of the household. "The man isn't perfect, but he's yours." That's something else the village women had said.

Two years later she'd awakened in the same way in the same room, on a straw mat next to her parents' bed. She had the mat to herself then, since a space for Pedro opened up when Jesús-the-second found a job near Teacapán, working as a gardener in a small gringo colony. Luz was fourteen, and the younger men were beginning to stare at the front door of Jesús Santos's house. Sometimes they talked to her at village fiestas. She kept her eyes downward most of the time while they talked, but not all of the time. Luz was different, which was a third thing the village women had said.

Luz had been fortunate in one way, since a spasm of educational reform provided the local school with teachers who could take her all the way through sixth grade. No farther, but at least that far. By Mexican village standards that was good. Her brothers had never gone beyond fourth grade, except for Jesús, who completed five years before he'd gone to work for the gringos near Teacapán to bring money back home.

Jesús-the-elder had spoken to her mother, saying grade three was enough for a girl, saying also too much education made women difficult to handle and a husband for Luz would be that much harder to find. Luz's mother had argued with him and said Luz was special, that she had dreams and should go as far as the teachers could take her. For such insolence Esmeralda Santos was beaten, but she was stubborn about it, and Luz was allowed to continue in school. She'd learned to read and write and studied basic Mexican history, a history colored by emotion and not entirely accurate, but no worse than colored-up history anywhere. She'd also learned to hunch her shoulders and bend a little forward when passing the village men, hiding in that fashion her breasts, which already were large and seemed to grow more so every day.

The other village girls were envious when a gringo photographer had visited Ceylaya and had chosen her for a series of portraits. He'd followed her into the fields and photographed her in her straw hat and feed-sack dress. And later a package had arrived with a picture of her, neatly matted and framed in silver. The photograph showed her standing, with the sea wind whipping her light dress about her legs and bending the brim of her hat. She was barefoot and smiling in a shy way back over her shoulder at the camera. The quiet, long-haired man in khaki shirt and orange suspenders had also smiled when he'd finished, lowering his camera and saying what he had just done would make a nice photograph of her and that he would send a copy. She kept the photograph as one of her prized possessions, a reminder of her village days.

Cholera — first from a traveler's hand, then from water or fruit — blew north. It had taken Luz's mother, then her father, then one of the middle boys. Luz escaped the disease, and the decision was clear: stay or go. Two young men in the village had needed wives, and everyone said Luz was a good catch; she not only had beauty but also knew how to work. Her only flaw was intelligence coupled with a slightly rebellious nature, but a few good beatings and seven or eight children would smother those qualities. As the men liked to say, "If they are pregnant, they will not wander." And machismo demands they do not wander — always, always, there is the fear of a woman giving favors to another man, for that is as bad as things get for *un hombre macho* married to the woman.

In the same gringo colony where he worked as a gardener, Jesús found Luz a maid's position in an American's house. She was fifteen and worked as hard as she did at home. But there was more food, and she was given shoes and a uniform and a bed of her own over the garage in a room she shared with two other young women. At night, she could hear the Pacific waves slapping the shore only fifty yards west of where she lay.

When the American's son had visited on holidays, he'd noticed Luz, noticed the fine legs and prominent breasts showing beneath her uniform, the pretty face with only the slightest hint around the eyes and high-cheeked facial structure of Indian blood left from generations back. The son was called David, and he was her first man. That he and Luz were swimming together at night and doing other things was understood by all, understood and accepted. David's father had worried about disease, so the boy always used a condom.

David was seventeen and clumsy, but Luz hadn't known any different and presumed such things lasted no more than the thirty seconds the boy made them last until his breath came fast and he lay still upon her afterward. Her mother had said it was the man's prerogative and whatever the man did was the right thing. But that's not what the images in magazines implied, not what the television soap operas suggested. The magazines and television made it clear that wearing fancy dresses showing off your woman's body was permitted, that it was all right to smile and speak unafraid in the presence of men. The stories said there should be moments of abandon in which the woman reached ecstatic heights of her own. It was all very confusing.

But David was a decent boy, and the family was decent overall, better than Luz had been taught to expect of gringos. They'd tutored her in basic English, good English, American colloquialisms included. Everyone said learning English was the key to better jobs in places where the tourists went. Climb the language hierarchy, get fluent, and you could become a hotel clerk or work in a shop where the gringo women purchased beachwear and Mexican clothing they toted back home and wore at garden parties.

At eighteen Luz had taken her things, become a gypsy for a day, and had ridden the bus to Puerto Vallarta. It was said a million tourists a year came to that exotic place and work was available for those who could speak English well. It was also whispered that once in a great while a gringo would take a young Mexican woman back to *el Norte* with him, back to the good life. From chambermaid at the Sheraton to assistant cook at La Plazita, that was the route for Luz, living those days with five other young women in a hillside shack. She would have stayed longer at the

Sheraton, but the assistant manager would not leave her alone, saying if she wasn't nice to him, she wouldn't have a job much longer. He was fat and ugly and had thick fingers that touched her when she walked by. La Plazita had a clean kitchen, at least.

The young gringo men who came in groups to Puerto Vallarta had money, more money than she could imagine. If you sat along the Malecón and smiled at them, they sometimes stopped and talked, saying, "Jeez, your English is pretty good," among other things. They wore T-shirts with obscenities printed on them and other ones saying, "Life Is a Beach," a metaphorical word-play Luz didn't understand at first, and they wore floppy shorts showing off their hairy, muscular legs. But they had paid twenty dollars for a night with a young Mexican woman, a cheap enough price for bragging rights back at Texas A&M.

Twenty dollars had been Luz's top body-price, since other young women had the same idea. And in Puerto Vallarta a twelve-year-old girl could be rented for only three dollars a night, cash paid directly to the girl's mother, who handed over the girl or brought her to a specified place. Guaranteed virgins ran a little higher. Danny eventually had told her about a bloated gringo who bragged around

Las Noches about being the first to take one of the young girls. The man had laughed when he let everyone know she wasn't large enough to handle him, how he'd torn her up and sent her back to her mother, who'd then had to find a doctor to staunch the bleeding.

Luz had whored only when she saw a new dress in a shop window or a nice pair of shoes she wanted. Not that it was a question of essential morality by this time, just that the whole business was fairly boring and not very refined, besides. There wasn't much to it, not all that different from the boy David. You played nice, drank a little something with them, and it was soon finished in one of the little hotels south of the Río Cuale. It was a practical matter, nothing more. They'd usually leave as soon as they were finished, but Luz would stay in the room all night since it had been paid for and there was hot water and a little privacy of her own for a while. None of them had said anything about taking her to *el Norte*.

When she was twenty and working at La Plazita, one of the busboys was ill on a Tuesday evening. Along with her work in the kitchen, Luz helped clean tables that night, something she ordinarily was not allowed to do. The gringo who came in was tanned and carried only a little belly, not as tall as some of them — perhaps five ten or so — and he had a pleasant face and nice brown hair hanging just over his shirt collar. She noticed the hair had a few streaks of gray in it.

He'd scratched his chin and ordered enchiladas, thinking she was there to take his order, but only men were allowed to be waiters. Before the waiter came, she whispered that the chiles rellenos were better, so he'd decided on that and asked her if she'd like to have an ice cream later. She'd said she would, and moved in with Danny Pastor two weeks later, heaven for a village girl. His apartment was small, but it had running water and a bathroom and a bed and closet. All of that plus a refrigerator and a stove.

Danny had known about making true love, more than Luz knew, but that didn't lay claim to much. Still, he'd been married and had read books on it. He told Luz he wanted to please her in bed, to bring her happiness, and taught her how to use her hands and mouth on him. The first time he put his tongue on her she tore the bed apart with pleasure and learned to scream into a pillow so the neighbors wouldn't hear. If truth usually lies somewhere in the middle of all continuums, it seemed in this case the magazines and television knew more than Esmeralda

Santos and the other villagers about men and women and the things they do with one another. Besides, Mexican men preferred that their wives remain ignorant of the erotic arts, afraid, as they said, "she might get to like it too much." Those were good things for mistresses or other bad women to know, but not wives, who might then seek out even more distant frontiers.

Danny had bought her three cassette tapes by María Conchita Alonso, whose love songs were popular with the younger women. He also had bought her two tapes by Pedro Infante to play on his battered tape player, since she still liked the old *música ranchera* she'd heard as a girl in Ceylaya. And also two tapes of salsa music by a guitar player called Ottmar Liebert, looking on the album cover as very close to a young Marlon Brando and playing rhumbas with just a touch of mariachi woven into them. When Ottmar Liebert played "La Rosa Negra," that one especially, was when Luz would dance a lickerish, naked rhumba for Danny. Danny, grinning and lying back on the bed and spilling tequila on the sheets and shouting, "God, let it all run forever!"

In the evenings, if Danny had money, they would go uptown and listen to Willie and Lobo in Mamma Mia. María de la Luz Santos had been born for this sweet life, and she wanted even more of it. Though it could get a little over the edge if you weren't careful. Such as the night Danny had been hanging all over a blond woman from San Diego. Just to show him, Luz went off to someone's yacht, where three men practically drowned her in tequila. She didn't remember much about it, except she was very sore in her lower parts for days. She never did that again.

The abortion had been a hard, hard thing for her, though it was common enough in Mexico among women of all classes, even those who considered themselves good Catholics. There was, first of all, the idea of family, drilled far and deep into a young girl's soul by a mother who could not see beyond that. And the village priest had railed against abortion — murder, he said it was. Above all, however, was the sense she wanted the child, wanted motherhood, and wanted Danny for a husband, even though he was nearly twenty years older than she.

But, after her wild night on a harbor yacht, Danny wouldn't hear of it, wouldn't think about having a child in any case, and she was afraid of losing what she had with him. So Luz had submitted to the abortion on a hot July day. She'd tried to forget it and after a while did forget it most of the time, yet the thought of it sometimes would come back to her, dwelling within her like a tack in the soul. Even after a year or two, she would cry when she remembered that summer morning. Afterward that same day, Danny had bought her a new Panasonic tape player. He'd also made sure she had plenty of birth control pills and made just as sure she took them.

Slowly she'd repressed thoughts of the abortion and got back to the way things were meant to be. When Danny's checks had arrived, they'd driven to Bucerías and eaten lobster and afterward driven out to Punta de Mita and swum naked in moonlit surf. Then one evening a curious thing had happened in the bar of El Niño, and later on that same night she rode in the Bronco named Vito, running hard with Danny and another man, running toward *el Norte,* where she'd always wanted to go and where Danny would never even talk about taking her.

In That Kind of Place

In late afternoon, heading due north on Route 15, Danny, Luz, and the shooter came up a long, high hill in heavy traffic, heat enveloping the Bronco as if they were riding through a brickyard kiln. At the top of the hill, Vito heated up and boiled over. Danny pulled off and inventoried the water supply, cursing himself for not bringing more. They'd been drinking water at a high rate, and there wasn't enough left to get Vito cooled down and moving again.

A Buick with Iowa plates was coming south and stopped. Leaning out the passenger-side window, a brown dog with white markings on her face panted and looked at them. An older gentleman with an "LSU Tigers" cap on his head leaned out the other window and asked if he could be of help. Danny said he could use some water if the man had any to spare.

"Sure do. It's in the trunk."

The man got out to open the trunk, and the dog followed him. While Danny was topping off the radiator, the shooter squatted down and petted the dog. "She got a name?" he asked of the older gentleman.

"Bandida. She's not much to look at, but she's got a lot of heart." Pretty bad cut on the man's face, he noticed.

"Bandida . . . that's a good name."

"Yep. Found her in New Orleans. She was in bad shape, living down by the waterfront." He glanced at the pretty Mexican woman sitting in the back of the old Bronco.

"Thanks," Danny said. "I think we're all right now."

"No bother." The older gentleman grinned. "Think I'll get on down the road. Retired a while back, and me and Bandida are visiting all the little beach towns. Got a lady librarian friend flying in from Otter Falls, Iowa, to meet me in Puerto Vallarta in a few days. If you ever need some good reading about travel, I'd recommend getting this." He held a book out the window, *Collected Essays on the Road Life*, written by someone named Michael Tillman.

The shooter smiled, Danny smiled, and the Buick moved south toward little beach towns and whatever else lay farther down in the belly of Mexico.

Relentless heat. Sun melting the highway tar patches and beating on the earth and reflecting off big water to the left, some kind of estuary or lake. A few miles farther on, Danny had to pee and swung across the highway onto a graveled turnout, parking Vito on the crest of a high bluff dropping off to the water below.

Danny went into the bushes, and when he came out the shooter was standing near the edge of the bluff. Luz was sitting on the ground, leaning against the Bronco's front bumper, long-billed fishing cap shading her eyes.

The shooter pointed out and down to the water, putting his other hand to his face, checking to see if the bleeding had stopped. It had.

"They're using nets," he said.

Half a dozen small boats were working the estuary stretching a mile either side of them and as far as they could see in the direction of the Pacific. One of the boats, the color of faded turquoise, was about a hundred yards from the cliff. A man in the bow cast a net out in front while another sat in the rear, tending a small motor. Water clinging to the net caught sparkles of sunlight when it fanned out.

"Fishing would be a good thing to do for a living," the shooter said. He said only that and watched the fisherman tossing the net and retrieving it in the old, old rhythms of fishermen everywhere.

Gravel crunched behind them, big-tire kind of crunch. The truck was a red Chevy Suburban, and Danny goddamn near fainted. *Federales* drove those vehicles after they'd confiscated them from dope dealers. That was his first thought, and he was right. Three of them got out. Two had .45's hanging from shoulder holsters outside their shirts; the other carried an automatic weapon of some kind on a strap over his right shoulder. Danny didn't know much about those things, but later the shooter said it was an Uzi, vicious little Israeli machine gun.

The *federales* looked mean and arrogant swaggering toward them, wearing Stetsons and expensive cowboy boots with a thin layer of dust over the shines. The one carrying the Uzi had a half-smoked cigarette in his mouth, ash dangling. Big one on the left, fat one, was hitching up his pants.

Danny was thinking fast, thinking about excuses and explanations:

"We're just traveling around looking at your beautiful country."

Or: "My friend had his papers stolen in San Blas, but we're going to stop in Mazatlán and clear that up, get him some

133

new documents."

Or: "The woman is our guide."

All of it weak, pathetic. Panic wrenching his gut, Danny was remembering how right his ex-wife had been about drinking and making decisions. Only he didn't know how absolutely right she was until much later, such as that very moment.

The shooter, still wearing his ball cap and sunglasses, lit a cigarette and watched the *federales* come on. Danny was thinking about the shooter's knapsack in the Bronco and was glad it was there, out of reach.

This would take some explaining, some interpreting to make sure the language was just right. Danny looked at Luz. She moved over to stand beside him.

The *federales* stopped twenty feet away. All three of them looking at the shooter, watching him hard, as if they knew something. Maybe interested in the cut on his face. A tiny drop of sweat hung on the tip of his nose and he was tossing his silver lighter up and down in his left hand. That level of nonchalance seemed a little strange to Danny. The very act of tossing and catching would subtract from the way he must be concentrating. Later on, Danny would recall how lazy the shooter had looked at that moment, almost sluggish, like he was passing time, waiting for a bus or for a woman to get dressed and go out. Clayton Price, going into his bubble.

Inside Danny's head was a sound he couldn't identify, like something scratching at a door and wanting to be let in.

One of the *federales*, big handsome hombre with a thin mustache, said, "Papers," and held out his hand, palm up. He resembled the old film actor Gilbert Roland.

Danny understood that much Spanish and turned to Luz. "Tell them you're a Mexican citizen, my papers are in the Bronco, and Mr. Schumann had his stolen in San Blas, but we're going to fix it up when we get to Mazatlán."

They were hesitating, and the *federales* could see that. The one who'd been doing the talking reached over to his left shoulder and unsnapped his holster. His .45 automatic had a pearl handgrip with little diamonds, or something that passed for diamonds, embedded in it. The diamonds reflected the sun, sending out bounces of light whenever the man shifted his body. Christ, what a cliché — diamond-studded pistol handgrip — something right out of a grade-C drive-in movie. Danny was drifting, the whole affair switching from what had seemed at the start like a controllable melodrama to something immeasurably real and nasty. He started thinking about Mexican jails and everything he'd heard about them: bad things, perdition on earth, maybe worse.

Luz said what Danny had told her to say, sweet voice, trying her best. The *federales* were not convinced, not even close to it. The fat man looked at the one who'd asked for papers and shook his head slowly back and forth. It wasn't going to work, Danny could see that, and he could almost smell the urine and rotting food in a Mexico City jail or the gray-stone prison just south of Mazatlán. God, set me free, get me out of this.

The shooter was still tossing his lighter up and down, relaxed and untroubled as far as anyone could tell. He stared at the *federales* while speaking quietly to Danny. "Will money do it?"

Luz looked at Danny, then at the shooter, then at the *federales*. She was terrified, her eyes showed it.

"I don't think so, but I'll try."

Danny told Luz to ask them if there was some nice way they could settle this business right there on the road. Maybe buy them some cold beer for their troubles. In a lot of situations that would have worked. Not this day. Danny could see the nasty expressions on their faces while Luz was making the offer. They were looking for someone, there was that sense of it, and one of the gringos before them didn't have any papers. Reason enough to haul all three of them in. Even though the *federales* operated as a law unto themselves most of the time, they'd be in deep trouble if they let somebody important, such as a hit man, get by them for the price of a case of beer. They weren't taking any chances.

Luz translated, "He says no, we must go with them and any more attempts to bribe an officer of the state will make things worse for us." Her voice was shaky, and Danny didn't blame her for being scared. Jail would be insufferable for him, much worse for a juicy señorita who was obviously loose in her ways just by virtue of her traveling with two gringos. A fly crawled up the sleeve of her white blouse and onto her shoulder. A few strands of long black hair were sticking to the perspiration on her neck, a few others blowing in a light wind off the estuary. She didn't move.

Break in the highway traffic . . . silence . . . then the sound of a boat motor far out in the estuary and birds singing in trees across the road.

Danny had no idea what to do next. He was absolutely stone-dead dumb, rooted there in repulsive spaces, as if some force had nailed his entire being to the ground and shrouded him in curious languor. He could sense his entire system shutting down, becoming indifferent, preparing for surrender.

Gilbert Roland pointed over his shoulder with his thumb. "This way. Leave your car here. It will be sent for."

Danny understood the words, but Luz translated anyway, sounding a long way off, like a frightened little girl who'd fallen down an abandoned well.

The shooter tossed his lighter, dropped it, and squatted down to pick it up. While he was squatting, he decided to tie one of his desert boots and pulled up his right pant leg a little in the process.

The heavyset *federale* started walking back to the truck, while the one who'd been doing the talking barked, *"Now."* He was out of patience and not about to acquire a new supply of it. The man with the Uzi swung it up, holding it easylike in his hands, watching Luz and Danny, disinterested in a man tending to shoelaces.

He got it first, the man with the Uzi. In the face. Blood exploding from a place two inches left of his nose.

Shooter yelling, "Down!" and running in a low crouch. Man with .45 reaching for pearl and diamonds. Didn't make it — two shots in the chest while his hand was on the way. Falling backward. Lying there . . . not dead, hands oaring the dust.

"Oh, sweet Lord, no . . . no . . . no." Danny was half thinking that, half saying it. All the time rolling-crawling toward the Bronco, dragging Luz with him. She was making little sounds equivalent to the ones Danny was making. Hanging on to him. Him on to her.

Fat hombre who went behind the Suburban — where'd he go? He came out fast. Double-barreled shotgun leveled and ready. Came out fast, but too slow, much too slow. No target he could see. The shooter was already behind the Suburban on the other side. Single shot from rear of truck. Shotgun man crumpled, crimson spray coming out of his ear. Over . . . over that fast. The *federales* did not get a shot off.

The shooter was breathing hard, but he never stopped moving. Danny was amazed at his strength and efficiency, particularly for an older guy. He walked quickly back to where the main *federale* was flopping around and holding on to his chest with one hand, trying to get his still-holstered pistol out with the other. The shooter stood over him, pointed the gun at the man's forehead and hesitated for a moment, then squeezed the trigger. The *federale* jerked once and lay still.

"Pastor," he shouted. "Get out from under the Bronco and get over here. Help me load these shitheads into the Suburban."

Danny crawled out and half stumbled over to where the shooter was standing over what had once been a Gilbert Roland lookalike but now had a dark hole in the forehead. They loaded all three of the *federales* into the rear of the Chevy and slammed the back doors, hearing the whine of a big diesel coming up the hill and around the curve north of them. The shooter jammed the gun in his belt, underneath his shirt, and scuffled dust over bloodstains on the ground. He finished and leaned against the Suburban just as the semi came around the curve. The driver waved to the tourists, the shooter waved back, grinning the grin of friendly American tourists everywhere, watching the truck go on down the road.

He stopped grinning and looked at Danny. "Where's the nearest Pemex station? Quick, think now."

Danny was having trouble thinking, except for his random and chaotic images of what had just happened and what it could lead to. Finally he said, "If I remember right, there's one up ahead, just south of Mazatlán, near the Durango turnoff."

The shooter nodded. "You drive the Suburban. Luz and I'll take the Bronco. When you get to the station, park around in back, as if you're leaving it there to be serviced. Then walk real slow over to the Bronco and get in the driver's side."

All at once and somehow they were heading up the highway toward Mazatlán, the shooter grinding gears, Luz's cap lying behind them along the road, where it had fallen off while Danny was dragging her under the Bronco. The shooter, one hand on the steering wheel, leaned over and reached in his knapsack, brought out an ammunition clip, and palmed it into the small black automatic with "Beretta" stamped on the barrel. He shoved the pistol back in his leg holster and, while he drove, began reloading the clip he'd used on the *federales,* all the while watching the tail of the Chevy up ahead.

It had been strange before, now it was getting chimerical in Danny's mind. The little caravan moved on toward Mazatlán, Danny watching his mirrors, seeing the Bronco a half mile back and smelling the sweat on the dead men in the space behind him. Dead men don't sweat — it sounded like a bad novel he might have read years before — but they sweat before they're dead, and ten

141

minutes ago they weren't dead. It had come down to survival, now. All that bullshit about writing a profile of a hit man seemed distant and, in that distance, naive. Tough reporter, hard-nosed journalist . . . Christ, what a joke. Compared with the man who was following him in Vito, the street punks of Chicago were still riding night buses from Dubuque to Peoria in the class D league.

South of Mazatlán, Danny pulled slowly into the big gas station complex and did as the shooter had told him. It was getting on in the afternoon, rush time at the Pemex, long lines of vehicles waiting for fuel and attendants hurrying. After parking the Suburban, he pretended a casual walk to the Bronco and got in behind the wheel.

Looking up from the map, the shooter said, "Take the Durango turnoff we just passed, head east into the mountains. Luz, you keep watching out the rear, anything strange looking comes up, say so." He turned back toward her to make sure she'd heard him. She bobbed her head up and down in acquiescence, hesitant and uncertain but swinging around to watch the road falling away behind them.

The shooter was a long way from home and in trouble. Danny had the feeling Peter Schumann or whoever he was had been in that kind of place before — in trouble and a long way from home. Now he and Luz were in that place, and they'd never been there, ever, not like this, anyway. Danny was trying to think clearly but couldn't. Instead, he focused on the road and listened to the rubber tires humming down the pavement and kept repeating to himself, "No . . . no . . . no." He said it over and over in his mind until it took on the slow, persistent drone of a mantra.

Felipe

Nothing from the field, from the roadblocks around Puerto Vallarta, or from farther out. Nothing from the car rental agencies or bus depots or airport. Walter McGrane sighed and knew it was coming down to the streets, to old-time detective work. He and the police chief in Puerto Vallarta mapped it out, starting with the bars and restaurants.

Confronted by hostile police and a young, hard-looking gringo in a windbreaker who did most of the talking in competent Spanish, the proprietor of El Rondo told what he knew. Felipe looked at the picture of Clayton Price and nodded. Yes, the tall gringo with the gray hair had stopped by for a drink two nights ago. Yes, he'd left with another gringo and a Mexican woman, both of whom he thought he'd seen before but whose names he didn't know. He described the gringo who'd been with the woman and started to tell how she'd sucked on her ice cream, but the men weren't interested in the woman's eating habits. So Felipe simply said she was very pretty and could speak English.

144

A Thing on the Mantel

Danny made the Durango turnoff and headed east through the late afternoon. The shooter looked straight ahead, chain-smoking Marlboros, his khaki shirt dark gray from sweat. Luz and Danny were a mess, sweat and red brown dust mixed together and sticking to their clothes and skin and hair. Luz had peeled her elbow in the scramble for safety while the shooter was taking down three *federales,* and she was pouring water on the abrasion, using a rag to wipe off the blood. The shooter glanced back, saw what she was doing, and handed his tube of ointment over the seat to her.

Danny, thinking. Decisions again and a single yardstick by which the choice set would be measured: survival. The old choice of stay or go, abandon or dig in. He and Luz could try to escape or somehow let the police know what was happening, maybe plead they'd been kidnapped. If the cops looked into things, however, and tracked them back to Las Brisas, plenty of people could testify there hadn't seemed to be any hint of them being captive. They might recall the separate rooms, the shooter swimming in the pool while he and Luz sat nearby, the easy talk over drinks and dinner. His other option was to help the shooter get out of Mexico and pretend he and Luz had never been part of anything other than a little trip north to visit her parents' graves.

What did anyone know so far? Danny ran the totals. In Puerto Vallarta, one man dead for sure and another wounded or dead. Crazy gringo and his girlfriend took off in the middle of the night, headed for somewhere. Nothing too unusual there, since crazy gringos did that sort of thing all the time. Three *federales* missing; the estuary fishermen might have heard the shots and maybe saw part or all of what happened on the bluff. If they had, chances were they'd look the other way and wouldn't report it, knowing they'd probably get in trouble of some kind just for being good citizens. They'd talk about it among themselves, though, and word eventually would get to the law. But in spite of what had occurred so far, the upside was nobody really had a fix on the three of them at the moment. Back to options, back to survival. Where did that leave him and Luz?

The shooter took over, closing down the

choice set. "Here's the drill, padre. You get me to the border or otherwise out of trouble, and I keep my mouth shut just like you're going to do, now and forever after, no matter what happens. No stories about this little adventure, Danny-the-sometime-writer, if that's what you're thinking. First Amendment rights have their limits, and I'm the limit right now and as far as you can imagine into the future.

"And let me tell you something else: We're not going to play the old movie game where I try to stay up nights and watch the two of you. That's the one where the bad guy eventually dozes off and everybody jumps him. This isn't make-believe. I'll sleep when I have to sleep. You'll do what you have to do. But if you're going to do something, get it right the first time; there won't be a second chance. You saw what happened back there. I'm looking for salvage now, don't care much about anything except getting out of Mexico. Got it?"

Danny glanced over at him. "Yes, I've got it." And he remembered again the wiseguys he'd dealt with back in Chicago. They were city tough and talked like it, dressed like it in flashy clothes, behaved that way — the Vitos and Sals and Vinnies. The shooter was different somehow. He seemed rather ordinary most of the time, quiet and pleasant, maybe lonely, almost pensive. But he could transform himself instantly into something else, something shadowlike and feral, something swift and implacable. As if you'd stepped into a dark room and were feeling your way through it, not seeing the fer-de-lance coiled on the mantel just at the level of your jugular, watching and waiting for your neck to come within range. The man who seemed lonely and quiet had been tying his shoe one moment, twenty seconds later three men who had stepped into a dark room on a sunlit road were dead.

"Good, you've got it. Now remember it," he said quietly. "Next, what's up ahead? The map says there's a town called Concordia."

Danny hesitated for a moment. The shooter was looking out the windshield and spoke without turning. "I'll say it again: Stop thinking whatever you're thinking — I get out of this, the two of you get out. It's not any more complicated than that. What am I going to have to deal with down the road?"

"East of Concordia there's an agricultural inspection station where they look for infected products. I remember it because of one thing: last time I came through, there were several men at the station, one of 'em was sitting in an office chair outside the kiosk, tilted back in the chair and holding some kind of mean-looking gun across his lap. I remember the office chair and the gun, particularly the gun. I thought that level of firepower was a little heavy-handed for an agricultural inspection station. Usually they just wave gringos on through, but they stopped me and poked around in my VW."

"When was that?"

"A little over three years ago. I think it was the old VW bus, why they looked me over. They associate those things with hippies and dopers."

"Long time. Things change. You remember anything about what type of gun the guy had?"

"I don't know, honestly. Had one of those curved clips attached to it. I guess they call 'em assault rifles."

"AK-47, probably. Who knows what's there now . . . something. If they were armed then, they're probably still armed. What's after that?"

"The mountains. Small villages along the way. Not all that much till Durango."

"How far to Durango?"

"Maybe a hundred fifty miles. Long haul, though, like I said before."

His nod was almost imperceptible. "We've got to get cleaned up before we go through that inspection station up ahead. We look like something that ought to be looked over carefully. Next creek we come to, turn off the road and drive up the creek out of sight."

Danny could see a cathedral spire slightly off to his left, five miles away. That'd be Concordia. The spire ascended through early evening light, soft light shining on the Sierra Madre wall forty miles straight ahead of them.

The shooter had a sense about things, and a creek came up a mile farther on, running shallow across the road. Danny did as he'd been told, checked to make sure no one was coming in either direction, and turned off the highway, following the water upstream. The creek was shallow with a rocky bottom, so he didn't bother with four-wheel drive. A quarter mile north the creek made a bend. Danny went around it and stopped when they were hidden from the road. The creek was in shadow there, cows grazing in a nearby pasture. Turkey vultures were perched in a tree upstream from them, a more obvious and pregnant symbolism than Danny cared to think about then or even later on.

As the shooter slid out of the Bronco, he looked at Luz and Danny, smiling a little. "In dry country, the path of flight which small birds take in the late afternoon usually leads to water . . . old survival rule."

The shooter took his denim shirt out of his knapsack along with rolled-up khaki pants, what he'd been wearing in El Niño when Danny had first seen him. He started for the water, then stopped and looked back to where Luz and Danny were still sitting in the Bronco, muddled and immobilized.

"Clean up. Both of you. We're going to look presentable when we hit that inspection station."

The shooter removed his shoes, shirt, and trousers, unfastened his leg holster and laid it on his clothing along with the sheathed knife. He was standing there in pale blue boxer shorts, his skin pale, too, except for his face and arms, a farmer's tan. And Danny noticed again the big, mean scars on his back and chest and thighs.

Danny pulled his duffel out and helped Luz get down from the Bronco with her cloth shoulder bag, which was more like a large purse. She was a mess, streaks of dirt on her face, dirt in her hair, on her clothes.

The shooter bent over and began to splash water on his face and chest, arms and legs. Danny waded into the creek a few yards above him, balancing himself against the poke of sharp rocks on his feet, and copied what the shooter was doing.

Luz went downstream a little and took off

her clothes. She wasn't particularly modest, never had been once she'd arrived at a certain point in her freedom, but not too much the other way, either. She stripped down to her underwear, pinned up her hair, and began slowly washing herself. After a while, she turned her back to the men and took off her bra and panties. In a place where the water deepened to six inches and ran smooth over gray sand, she lay down, resting on her elbows, the top third of her breasts showing above the water. The water ran around her breasts and over her belly and legs.

She lay there for perhaps thirty seconds before sitting upright again, the shooter watching her as he finished washing himself. She must have felt that somehow and half turned toward the men, one breast in full view. Danny was surprised to see her smile, a small enigmatic smile, but with a curious warmth to it, curious because of the circumstances. She turned away again and sat there, washing the dirty clothes she'd taken off.

Danny worked on the incongruity of it all: the gun, the killing, the fer-de-lance in the water near him, and the soft, brown woman who gently washed her body and clothing in a shadowed creek, on a warm evening in Mexico.

While the shooter dressed, he said, "Let's

stop playing this shell game. You saw me do the hit in Puerto Vallarta, didn't you?"

Danny stammered around a little, finally saying yes.

"I thought so. When I walked out of there I saw you watching me. It was no accident I drifted into that little bar where you were drinking tequila later on. After I left El Niño, I hid in a doorway on Calle Aldama. I wanted to get the hell out of there, but I also didn't want to take a chance on leaving you behind all full of tequila and talkative when the cops came. It was a tough decision, whether to wait for you or not. I gave myself three minutes, after which I'd have been gone. When you and Luz left, I followed you."

A chill raced up Danny's spine, bounced off some higher place above him, and came back down along its original track.

"You were after *me*, for God's sake?"

"Yes. I was waiting for the right street, somewhere quiet and dark."

"Were you going to kill both of us?"

"I wouldn't have had any choice."

"Why didn't you?"

"Well, sometimes I'm not very good at this, not anymore. In spite of what you may think, I'm not as hard as I once was. For some reason I've been fading a little as I get older. Ten years ago you'd both have been lying on the pavement in Puerto Vallarta." He was talking matter-of-factly, cold and flat, stating facts, not bragging. "Frankly, I looked at Luz sitting in . . . whatever that little bar is called, in her lavender dress, looking young and pretty and eating an ice cream, and couldn't bring myself to do it. You, I didn't care about, still don't if you're wondering."

Danny wasn't wondering and had no doubts whatsoever about where he stood in the overall picture.

"Then I got the idea of having you drive me to the border. The boat that was supposed to pick me up had been delayed, the usual foul-up, so I needed to get out of Puerto Vallarta anyway. Having you take me, I could keep an eye on you for a few days while the cops were running all over everywhere and find out at the same time if you'd seen anything in El Niño. That done, I'd have been over the border and a long way from here. If it came to it, I was going to take you down and just scare hell out of Luz, guessing she'd never say anything."

"Is that still an open course of action?"

"Depends on you, gringo."

"If I'd said I wouldn't take you to the border, what would have happened?"

The hard smile Danny had seen before came at him again. The shooter didn't say anything. He didn't have to.

Two hours before full dark, they left the creek and got on the road again. Luz was wearing a red blouse and clean jeans. Danny was in jeans and a plain gray T-shirt. The shooter had put on his photographer's vest over the denim shirt.

Danny took them through the edge of Concordia, took them slow, not wanting to swivel any attention their way. Dust of the day going down, kids playing, men sitting in roadside restaurants while women laughed and cooked chicken over wood fires, smoke rising and blowing off on the evening breeze. They rolled past roadside stands where handmade furniture was for sale, craftsmen making it and selling in open-air shops, working under thatched roofs supported by poles.

Luz was on her knees, balancing herself with one hand on each of the two front seats. As they went by the furniture shops, she spoke quietly. "It is every village woman's dream to own one of those fine beds in which she can lie and conceive and give birth."

To Danny, her words and the way in which she'd said them seemed a curious thing at that very moment. A kind of peasant's lamentation with undercurrents, as if she were thinking of other routes she might have taken,

155

as if she were grieving for the structure and traditions she'd abandoned when she left her village. Danny had always known there was a part of Luz that was still a *campesina* — a country girl — a good Catholic girl. It surfaced occasionally, and her speech turned almost nostalgic when it did.

The shooter turned and looked at her, his face only a few inches from hers, and stared at her for a long moment. He nodded, as if he understood what lay beneath her words, smiling in a way that, for him, seemed uncommonly genuine and warm. Luz smiled back at him.

"Inspection station's up ahead," Danny said.

The shooter turned from Luz and studied the road, reaching in his knapsack and dropping an extra clip for the Beretta in his left vest pocket.

"Roll up to it, easylike. Grin real wide and say, '*Buenas tardes.*' Keep rolling, though, as if you expect them to wave you right on through." He glanced back at Luz. "If we're stopped and things go bad, keep your head down."

Danny was wishing they were traveling in something a little more classy than the Bronco. Mexicans judged things by appearance, particularly people and what the people

156

drove. And they were driving suspicious-looking junk.

Fifty yards from the station Danny slowed the Bronco. Two men in uniforms were leaning against posts supporting an overhanging roof under which vehicles passed. A third was doing something behind the glass of the kiosk. The fourth and fifth men were armed. One had a revolver in a waist holster. The other carried a rifle similar to the one Danny remembered from his previous visit. Ugly gun, with a metal, hinged stock that was nothing more than a triangular bar, curved clip sticking out of the bottom of the rifle.

The shooter was talking through lips that barely moved, flexing the fingers on his right hand as he spoke. "The rifle's a Galil .308, holds twenty-five rounds, probably modified to be fully automatic . . . nasty little bastard. Wish I had it instead of him. Probably hasn't been cleaned in two years."

For a moment Danny thought they were going to be waved through. Just as he was about to accelerate, the man wearing the pistol held up his hand, signaling for them to stop. The shooter was coming up to combat status; you could feel it, could almost hear his adrenaline escalating.

He let out a long, slow breath and talked

low. "Everybody smile. We're just dumb tourists from Mazatlán out here wandering around."

Given the condition of the Bronco, Danny had his doubts about the plausibility of that explanation, but he couldn't think of anything better.

"Buenas tardes," Danny said.

The pistol man said good afternoon back to him and bent over, looking in at Vito's occupants. He stared for a few seconds at each of their faces. "You have fruit or vegetables?"

Luz said they did, showing him apples and oranges that were getting rough after two days in the heat.

The inspector said nothing, then looked at the shooter and smiled. "Bad scrape, amigo," tapping his own face when he said it. "Trouble?"

The shooter may or may not have understood. He grinned back at the inspector, then shrugged and turned toward Luz, handing the conversation over to her.

"He fell while we were climbing rocks along the coast." Luz was giving the man her very best come-along-and-see-what-I-have smile while she spoke. She glanced at the shooter and switched to English. "The rocks along the coast were very slippery,

158

weren't they, causing you to fall and hurt your face."

The shooter pointed at his wound, still grinning, then tightened his face into a grimace and said, "Oww . . . very sore, very dumb thing to do," shaking his head gently from side to side, playing the ignorant gringo who didn't understand how treacherous sea rocks could be. Watery theatrics, but they seemed to do the job.

The man looked at him again, then smiled and spoke passable English. "You must be more careful, amigo. Mexico is a dangerous place for those not used to it."

He straightened up and swept his hand forward, motioning for them to proceed. Danny let out the clutch easy as he could and gradually accelerated toward the Sierra Madre. In the mirror, he could see the pistol man standing with his hands on his hips, watching them move away. A few moments later, as he'd been instructed to do, the man went inside the kiosk and picked up a telephone.

Foothills of the Sierra Madre. Piedra Blanca, Magistral, Guasima, Zapotillo — villages not on any map, but nevertheless straddling the road or lying a few clicks to one side.

The shooter said, "Good job back there,

both of you. Now, we need a place to lay up for a day or two, get a feeling for how serious the hunters are. Pretty serious, I'm guessing. We'll stand out too much in these villages, word'll get passed around about us hanging out. Am I right or wrong about that?"

"Pretty much right," Danny told him. "Every village has what we'd think of as a local cop, a constable. He won't be armed and won't bother us directly, but it's his job to notify other law about any unusual goings-on in his village. Eventually the police drive up to the village and take a look for themselves. Sometimes they let a week go by before they get around to it. With all that's happened, however, they might respond right away. We'll stick out, no doubt about that."

"Any ideas?"

"Up the road about sixty miles is a place I've heard about, called Zapata. Friend of mine hung around there for a couple of weeks a while back. It's quaint, been turned into a minor tourist stop. Buses haul tourists up from Mazatlán for a few hours, let 'em eat and take a walk. They go back home and say they've been to a traditional Mexican village. There's some kind of place to stay, cantina or two, maybe a restaurant. A few gringos live there permanently from what I understand, so we won't be quite as noticeable as in some of these other places."

"Let's take a look at it."

Around a curve, hombre on a chestnut horse coming the other way, riding on the edge of the road. Mustache and goatee, aristocratic and handsome in the face, black vest and pants, white shirt open at the neck, black flat-crowned hat and black boots, saddle inlaid with silver. An apparition coming out of a lavender evening. He watched them pass, then moved down the road. Mexico . . . that way: garbage and cruelty, beauty and surprise, nobility on a horse in the middle of nowhere.

Seventy-five minutes later and a mile west of Zapata, the Bronco began jerking and made weird, threatening noises under the hood.

The shooter came to attention. "What's that?"

Danny was hunched over the wheel, looking at gauges. "Don't know, sounds bad."

They limped up to the Zapata turnoff, rolled down into a deep valley on the edge of the village, then began climbing again. Up front the noise got louder. The Bronco gave signs of stopping completely, leapt forward a few feet, halted for a moment, then jerked and humped its way up the hill. They made it to the top and sputtered along narrow cobblestone streets, making a not-so-grand entrance into the central plaza area of the village.

The plaza was square and thirty yards on a side, with a gazebo in the middle and lots of trees. A cobblestone street circumscribed the plaza and separated it from buildings on all four sides. On the south a huge old church rose up and dominated everything. Beyond the church were mountains, and valleys in evening shadow. To the west was a long, single-story building divided into individual residences, with a little shop at the south end near the church. The east side was mainly a combination curio shop and residence about forty feet long. On the north was what they were looking for, a tourist version of a cantina and a restaurant advertising rooms for rent.

Danny stopped the Bronco and looked around. A few teenage couples were involved in temperate courting rituals around the plaza. Old men tilted back in chairs against the outside walls of their houses, staring at the gringos who'd just staggered in. Vito was sounding as if death were imminent, so Danny lurched it behind the restaurant, spooking a wandering burro, and shut down. The Bronco died with a rattle in its throat.

The streetlights on all four corners of the plaza came on, and Zapata, indeed, looked quaint and picturesque at night. Electricity had arrived, which was surprising, since most of these villages didn't have it yet. Later on, Danny would hear Zapata was the home village of Mexico's former president and had been favored because of that. He slumped over the steering wheel, watching bugs fly around street lamps. The three of them sat there for a moment, saying nothing, letting down from a strange, violent day. San Blas and the swimming pool at Las Brisas seemed as if they were in another time, another universe, yet they'd been there only this morning.

Three chickens walked by, pecking at whatever chickens find nobody else can see. The burro had moved up the street and stood there, looking back over its shoulder at them.

The shooter let out a tired breath. "Let's find a place to stay. Luz, you go in and check things out."

"I'd better go with her," Danny said. "This place smells gringo to me, and they may refuse her."

"You mean a Mexican in a Mexican village would refuse a Mexican woman a room?"

Danny couldn't tell if he was being skeptical about the two of them going off by themselves or if he was genuinely incredulous.

"Yeah, if they're catering to tourists, they

just might do that. To a lot of Anglos all Mexicans are wetback labor who just happen to be living south of the border instead of bending low in the vegetable farms of the San Joaquín. And the white folks ain't sharing toilets with wetbacks if it comes to that."

"For chrissake . . . go do it."

The shooter was obviously tired and should have been and wasn't making any attempt to hide it. In the last eight hours he'd kicked hell out of two hombres in a Teacapán beach joint plus carved three notches on his lifetime kill-total, and God only knew what that might be. Danny noticed the lines under his eyes were back again, deep and concentric and dark.

A plump, pretty Mexican woman was tending bar. Other than her, the place was empty in the middle of May, off season for the tourist trade. She told them they'd have to see the head hombre and fetched him.

He stood by the bar and looked them over, three days' growth of beard and rolling a toothpick across his lower lip with a bad nick in it. Danny couldn't tell if he was friendly or unfriendly or something in the middle. They asked to see a room, and he took them through the bar into a small courtyard serving as a dining area and up a narrow flight of stone steps. The steps led to a balcony over-

164

looking the courtyard, with a row of rooms to their left along the balcony.

The proprietor unlocked a door and swung it inward. A single overhead light hung from a cord, and the hombre flipped it on. The room was small, twin beds with serapes striped in Mexican colors draped across them and a wash basin on a stand. Plain, sparse, but clean and tidy, designed for low-budget gringo travelers. Ten dollars a night.

Danny told him they needed two rooms, another person was waiting in the car. The second room was a reprise of the first, with a single window in the rear and opening onto a tile roof with the street only a short distance below where the tile ended. Danny was guessing the shooter would be interested in alternate exits from anyplace he stayed.

They lugged their gear through the bar, across the interior courtyard, and up the stairs. On the way Danny asked the bartender about food. It was getting late, she'd have to check with the hombre again.

The shooter looked around his place, then knocked on the door of Luz and Danny's room. He said he was thirsty and told Danny and Luz he'd meet them down in the bar.

In their room, Luz put her arms around Danny. He did the same to her, and they stood there for what seemed like a long time, holding each other, not saying anything. Each knew what the other was thinking: they were in one hell of a fix.

"You okay, Luz?"

"I am frightened, Danny. But I cannot decide about this man. He is nice to me and kind, but he kills without sorrow or thought. He is like something I've never imagined. Like some black horseman the old people used to talk about, an avenging spirit who comes riding only on the darkest nights and takes people away without warning. But I think I am more frightened because of our situation than I am of him. In some ways I feel secure because of what he can do."

"We're in a tough spot, Luz. I don't know quite how we're going to get out of it. It's a goddamned casserole. I'm sorry I got us into it."

"Danny, did you know about this man when we were still back in Puerto Vallarta?" She rolled her *r*'s smooth and pretty, something Danny had never been able to make his tongue execute.

The side of her head was against his chest. "Yes, I saw him shoot those two men in the street. I was naive and stupid and arrogant enough to think I could pull this off, take him to the border and get a good story out of it. That's why I didn't want you to come along, but I couldn't argue too strongly with you. I was afraid he'd find out I knew something. I should've booted your sweet little ass right back in the house and let you pout about it."

As he was saying that, he was running his hand over the sweet little part of her and finally left it there. She felt warm in the way only María de la Luz Santos could feel, and he wanted her right then, something to push back the day and all that had happened.

But she pulled back a little and said, "He will be wondering what we are doing. We had better go down."

Luz took his hand, and they walked along the balcony, down the stairs, and through the courtyard lighted by blue and green bulbs strung diagonally across it. Of the ten bulbs, six were working. Of the six, a blue one was flickering.

He stopped for a moment and looked at her. "Luz, doesn't all this bother you, the killing, the violence? You seem pretty calm about it."

"There is a strength that comes from having been raised a peasant, Danny. You accept what is and what takes place as beyond your control. You work on getting through today and hoping tomorrow won't be any worse. When I was a young girl and would complain about something or other, I remember my mother saying, 'Luz María, happiness is impractical.' If he hadn't killed those *federales,* we'd all be in prison now. But we're not, and that's good. Things could be worse."

The shooter was leaning back in a chair with his feet on another chair. He'd finished a Pacífico and was starting on a second one, squeezing a wedge of lime into it. Danny ordered the same for him and Luz and poured down a third of the bottle on his first pull at it. The woman tending bar went off to find the main hombre and ask about food.

While Danny and Luz had been in their room, two gringos wearing dusty jeans and boots, snap-button shirts, and Stetsons had come in the cantina and were standing at the bar, drinking beer. One of the men kept looking back at the shooter, who pretended to be studying the walls but wasn't. The cowboys finished their drinks and walked toward the door.

The taller man stopped by the table, looked at the shooter, and spoke in a low Texas drawl, hoarse, as if loose stones were rattling around in his throat. "I know you? Seems I do, somehow."

The shooter raised his head and looked directly at the cowboy's eyes. "Don't think so; not that I recall, anyway."

168

"Thought I'd seen you before, somewhere, long time ago, 'Nam maybe."

"Don't think so."

"Sorry to bother you."

The cowboys went out on the porch, one of them talking in low, insistent tones to the other: "Jack, you've got to get your head straight. Linda's been gone a long time, and she ain't comin' back. Sharon's gone, Linda's gone, they're all gone, 'cause men like you and me are just too goddamn crazy to put up with." One of the men coughed badly as they walked into the night and climbed into a pickup. The sound of the truck faded as they headed out of Zapata and up onto the Durango road.

The shooter tilted his head toward the porch and said, "By what those two were saying, everybody's going or gone."

He took a drink of his Pacífico, then held up the bottle and studied it. "It's almost impossible to overstate the medicinal properties of beer."

Danny stared at him and wondered how he could sit upright, let alone drink beer. Christ, he looked tired, face sagging. The shooter took another hit of his Pacífico and wiped the back of his hand across his mouth.

"That guy seemed pretty sure he knew you," Danny said.

"Remember him from 'Nam — First Cav or Seventh Marines, someplace — tough hombre, if I'm remembering right. Didn't want to let on I recognized him, though."

There wasn't much to lose now, no secrets anymore, so Danny asked him straight out, "This what you call settling messy accounts, the whole business we're involved in?"

Clayton Price smiled a little. "That was Puerto Vallarta. The rest of it's just getting by and getting home."

"How long you been at this?"

The shooter finished his beer, went behind the bar, and got himself another, talking while he did it. "Since I was . . . let's see, twenty-eight . . . after I got out of Vietnam and out of the marines."

He returned to the table, riding on that easy, long-legged walk of his, and sat down, looking hard at Danny, who had the distinct sensation an electric drill was headed for a point just above his nose, the Doppler effect of the shooter's presence.

The shooter didn't say anything for a moment, straightened the bracelet on his right wrist, looked at it. Then: "It's a trade you learn, like anything else. I picked up the basic skills in the military, long time ago. Some people make furniture, some do what I do.

170

It's all a question of learning a craft and using tools."

Clayton Price held the bottle of beer against his face. "I was a sniper, one of a handpicked group of men whose job it was to harass the enemy. Legalized terrorism, in other words. We were good at it, too. One guy had ninety-three confirmed kills. In one particular month he killed thirty people from long range, one-third as many as an entire battalion did operating in the same area. The VC called him White Feather, after a feather he wore in his bush hat." The shooter shook his head in admiration. "I remember the time White Feather blew away one of Charlie's ace snipers, put a round right down the other guy's scope from a few hundred yards out. Damn, he was good, the best."

"How many did *you* have . . . kills?"

"Eighty-two, confirmed, couple hundred probables. The VC put a price on my head at about number fifty. Three years' pay to the man who got me."

"What's a 'probable'?"

"Meant there wasn't any officer or NCO around to put their stamp of approval on it."

"You killed eighty-two men in a war?" Luz almost whispered her words, shocked and disbelieving.

Clayton Price lit a cigarette and nodded, looked at her seriouslike. "Closer to three hundred. One at a time, and not all of them were men."

"Women, too?" She was incredulous.

He shrugged. "Sometimes children, if they were killing us in one way or another, and a lot of them did. They weren't children in the way you think of children. Charlie made them into full-blown soldiers, running around with grenades and bombs under their shirts. You wouldn't have heard too much about that, aside from the occasional massacre that made the news. Americans are so bloody innocent, or pretend to be; they wave flags and want war, but they want war with rules. There are no goddamned rules in the jungle. The Geneva Convention was a Stone Age document that had no relevance out there. Talk about contradictions — hollowpoint bullets and shotguns were banned by the so-called Law of Land Warfare, but it was apparently all right if the VC skinned people alive.

"And some of the women were more brutal than you can imagine. One in particular was famous for cutting off the genitals of captured pilots within shouting distance of our compounds, then turning them loose. They'd run toward our perimeter wire, naked, with nothing left between their legs and blood spurting like a faucet from where their genitals had been. So much for the Geneva Convention and rules of war. We eventually got her. I shot her at seven hundred yards while she was squatting down taking a pee. Her head exploded like a cantaloupe. Technically, four hundred yards is the maximum range for a sure head shot, so I zeroed in on her chest, but she lowered herself a bit just as I squeezed the shot off. It was a tough, cruel game. No quarter asked, none given. Still is, for that matter . . . still tough and cruel."

Danny was silent for a moment, wondering about a woman's head exploding like a cantaloupe, trying first to get the picture in his mind and, once he'd done it, trying to get rid of the image. "What does a sniper do? How did you work? My only image is one from old newsreels . . . Japanese with weeds sticking out of their helmets, perched in palm trees in the South Pacific."

"Different now, though the mission is similar — create fear, create ambiguity and indecision, make people afraid to step outside or poke their heads up."

Danny tried to see him in his bush hat, in the jungle, all those years ago, this man sitting across the table in a Mexican mountain village. He got the picture with no difficulty.

The shooter paused, lit another cigarette.

When the bartender came back, he signaled her he'd fetched a beer while she was out, making scribbling motions on his left palm to indicate she should put it on their tab. She got the message, then brought three plates of beans, rice, tomatoes, and cold chicken to the table. Luz started eating. Danny's stomach was feeling a little dicey, listening to the shooter equate heads and cantaloupes, watching him dig a fork into refried beans.

"So you just drifted out of the military and into becoming a . . ." Danny couldn't quite say it.

The shooter swallowed, smiled again, and filled in the blank. "A professional killer, you mean? An assassin, cloven hoofed and all the rest?"

"Whatever you call it."

"Don't be afraid of the word — it's called killing. I'm a sniper. From the guy with a crossbow in the bushes who knocked off Richard the Lion-Hearted, to Leonardo da Vinci picking off enemy soldiers from the walls of Florence with a special rifle he designed, to Jim the Nailer out in India, in the siege of the Lucknow Residency, we've always been here. We're what rises when things have gone too far, when law and politics have failed.

"There's a lot of gray areas out there; you

can be out of the military but still working for them or some government somewhere. Civilians don't like to believe that, but it's true. You transcend into freelancing . . . people call you. Very little, almost none, of my work has been the kind of thing you saw in Puerto Vallarta. That was a special project. Mostly I've worked as a mercenary, a soldier-for-hire, wherever there're bad guys."

"How do you define 'bad guys'?"

"Anybody who's not on my side."

Danny thought about that for a moment, then continued. "Where have you worked?"

"All over. There's always some nasty little war going on someplace. Or a remote drug lab in Colombia where the kingpin's visiting and somebody wants him taken out, things like that. Africa's been especially good over the years, and Latin America, the Middle East, too. I'm jungle trained, so I try to stay in those areas. Sniping is a specialty, that's what they hire me for. Usually to take out some general or politician. As I said before, same thing all snipers do: create fear, indecision, ambiguity — lock the important creeps close to home, keep 'em from moving around. I was on a plane headed for Baghdad once, dressed up as some kind of ambassador's assistant. Except I had a disassembled rifle and fifteen rounds of match-grade ammo in the diplomatic mail pouch. They called us back . . . don't know why."

He looked at the table, massaged his fingers. "That one would have been interesting. Insertion is relatively easy; extraction is where it gets hairy."

"You do any job, no matter what it is?"

"Most do, I don't. I have my standards." He stopped, grinned at Danny, then at Luz. "Sounds odd, doesn't it, a professional killer with standards? I don't get much work for the American government because I won't do a job without knowing the reason for it. Usually they won't tell you, but I won't work blind and stand firm on it. Tell me the reason or call someone else. That's why I like mercenary work, soldiering-for-hire . . . you generally have some idea of why the hell the war's being fought, and you can decide to join up or not, depending how you feel about the issues at stake. And I don't kill anything and call it sport, ever . . . animals included. Killing is not sport, it's killing, period, and I happen to do it for a living."

"What kind of jobs would you turn down?"

"Some rich guy wants his wife out of the way so he doesn't have to pay out big money when he divorces her. Or somebody's just mad at somebody else or wants a business partner removed. Things like that.

For a few hundred bucks, you can hire an eighteen-year-old ghetto kid to do that work. Don't get me wrong, I'm not making all of this seem honorable. Not trying to justify it. It's what I do, that's all, and I do it my way."

"What if somebody lied to you, about the reason for doing a job?"

"They know better than that." He took a drink of beer, and Danny believed his words.

"I'm surprised you did the shooting in Puerto Vallarta from such a public place as El Niño."

"Ordinarily I wouldn't. There's no code of honor in this business about how the job gets done. Do it at long range if you can — as we used to say in 'Nam, long range is the next best thing to being there. Long range, and in the back if possible. But never in public, not if you can help it. I'd been looking for that guy for a couple of weeks and was running out of time. I was sure he was still in Puerto Vallarta, but he was lying up somewhere and I couldn't find him. Suddenly he was there, getting out of a car right on the main drag. So, tying all of it together, it's a matter of getting a little old and getting a little careless and sometimes not giving a damn anymore for some reason.

Plus not having any other choice if the job was going to get done.

"I think I'm slipping a bit. Also, there's a lot of new high-tech weaponry out there I don't have easy access to and don't know how to use — night-vision glasses, sophisticated explosives. I'm pretty much a specialist, an old-time gunman, never have known much about explosives other than a few basic things. I'm starting to feel obsolete, like I've been flying close to the sun for a long time. Thinking now and then about closing down."

"The naval officer was a target, too?"

"Uh . . . that was something else; let's say he was a secondary target."

"Why were you sent to kill them?"

Clayton Price had finished his supper, and the blue gray eyes with dark circles under them looked at Danny, then down at the Pacífico beer. Luz had gone off to the rest room and the bartender was sitting on the porch, out of earshot.

"I have some things to tell you. You think it's been rough so far? It could get a lot rougher before this is over, so it seems like you ought to know the whole story. Not sure why, just seems that way." He looked off in the direction Luz had gone. "For her sake, maybe."

Danny took a drink of his beer and said nothing.

"The civilian I killed in Puerto Vallarta was preparing to sell computer secrets to a Taiwanese industrial consortium, something to do with something called failure analysis, some kind of sophisticated computer simulation of why things go wrong. The military is very interested in this technology. American business firms are hot on it, too. It's one of the next technological frontiers, and one of the few areas where Americans are ahead of the pack. When one of the big defense firms got its budget whacked in the current wave of military cutbacks, a number of high-ranking engineers were laid off. One of them was the civilian in Puerto Vallarta. He'd decided to pick up a tip on his way out and was selling what he knew about failure analysis to this Taiwanese group. His payoff was in the big millions, that was the rumor.

"The hit was contracted for by a branch of the U.S. government, not sure which one. There was a go-between, of course . . . there always is, but it smelled *government* right from the start, and I confirmed that before I signed on. I wasn't the only one hired, there were two or three other freelancers, that's how bad they wanted him. At least one other contractor was in Puerto Vallarta, saw him sitting in a bar one night. Knew he was a shooter. There's an old Russian proverb, 'A fisherman sees another fisherman from afar.' All of us were given carte blanche, go where we had to go, do what we had to do. We each were guaranteed a flat amount of money plus a bonus for the man who got the job done — bounty hunters.

"I was told the transfer of information might take place in Mexico, and I tracked this engineer to Puerto Vallarta. Couldn't find him once I got there. I knew he was going to meet someone soon, but I didn't know where or when. I was just sitting in El Niño one night, and there he was."

"But you had your gun under your vest on the windowsill. You must have had some idea he was going to show up."

"You stay ready. Strange things happen. Luck sometimes plays a part in it, in spite of what I said about luck the other night."

"What about the naval officer you shot?"

The shooter smiled in a sad way and scratched his right cheek. "Not sure why I'm telling you all this. Sometimes I don't seem to care much about anything anymore, I guess."

He sighed and stared up at the ceiling. "It gets pretty bizarre, about here. When I was in Southeast Asia, we were sent on a hush-hush mission to kill a Dutchman who had a plantation in Cambodia and apparently friends in high places. He was letting the Viet Cong use his plantation for a storage dump, and, believe it or not, he was an expert in torture. 'Don't get captured in that sector or the Dutchman will go to work on you and you'll wish you'd never been born while you're praying for death,' that was the word.

"Three of us went. A captain who was my commanding officer, my spotter, and me. We were rousted out of bed in the middle of the night, told to gather our equipment and go down to the helicopter landing area. Fifteen minutes later we were on our way. . . ." The shooter paused and smiled. "That cowboy that was just in here . . . he was a gunner on the chopper that took us out on the mission, but he didn't come back with the dust-off crew. Snipers are taught to be good observers, see everything and never forget it. Took me a few minutes, though, to realize where I'd seen him before. Damn, over twenty-five years ago and here he is drinking beer in little ol' Zapata . . . can you imagine that, right here in Zapata."

He shook his head and sat quiet for a moment, then went on. "Anyway, none of us had any idea of what was up on that particular mission; all I knew is that we were being sent to kill a special person somewhere. Even the captain didn't know. He was given a small piece of a larger map, covering only about five square miles, the area in which we'd be working. Found out later we were in Cambodia. When I asked the captain that night what the hell we were up to, he said, 'Same as always, peelin' tails and suckin' heads.' He was from the bayou country and liked to use that crawfish metaphor."

Danny was still dawdling with his supper but shoved the plate away when the shooter started quoting bayou philosophers.

"It was a precision operation, no room for error. We set up our 'hide' and waited, all three of us hunkered down there for almost four hours. Intelligence had somehow gotten word the Dutchman would be coming along a certain trail on his way to meet with the VC, did it every morning, apparently. Sure enough, he came out of the jungle two hours after dawn. Pith helmet, khakis, walking stick, the whole business. It was a relatively easy shot. I put a hollow-point in his throat at four hundred fifty yards, which probably did the job since his head fell over to one side and was barely hanging there by a few pieces of skin, at least it looked that way to me through the scope. But, by God, he got to his feet somehow and started running around all over the place, head flopping on his shoulder and blood spraying out of the wound. None of us had ever seen anything like it before, like a chicken after you've cut off its head. The captain said, 'Hit 'im again.' So I put another round dead between his shoulder blades . . . that took him down for good.

"Next thing we know, a mortar burst hits twenty yards from us. As careful as we'd been, someone had spotted our position. We took off running like hell down a gulch, then climbed a hill at least two hundred yards high. The deal was, the captain had called in a chopper that was to be at point X to pick us up in twenty minutes. Christ, there was suddenly VC all around us."

Danny watched the shooter's eyes widen at the remembrance of terror, of true and absolute fear and flight.

"Automatic weapons fire, mortars, all hell breaking loose. My spotter got cut right in two from a burst; I mean, there was nothing left of him, entrails slopping out, a mess. The captain and I kept running, scared as hell. We came over the top of the hill and ran down the other side, our clothes being ripped by thorns and God knows what else. My shirt was in rags. We came to this meadow, still running, but the VC cut us off. So we detoured across an open rice field, running along the dikes. We were damn near gone, stumbling, fighting to get air in our lungs.

"We could see the chopper coming in to pick us up about a half mile ahead. The pilot saw us running through the paddies and changed his landing zone, found a place, and set it down. The captain took a round when we were still two hundred yards away from the chopper sitting there with its blades turning. I got him up on me, piggyback style, and started off again. The VC were closing in from three sides, but I could see we were going to make it if the pilot would just wait. I'm knee deep in water and mud, the extra weight of the captain pushing me down, taking it one step at a time, churning, big sucking noises every time I lift a foot and take a step. There's a guy crouched in the chopper's passenger bay, door open. When we're only thirty yards out and the VC closing in, he panics, waves the pilot off, and the chopper leaves. I've always remembered his face looking down at me as they lifted off; it's been carved into my mind for all these years . . . his face. The sonuvabitching coward just left us there.

"Anyway, I'd been fishing around Puerto Vallarta for almost four days and nothing to show for it. I'm sitting there looking out the window of El Niño on a pleasant evening and who should come strolling down the street in his nice white uniform but the guy who left me standing there in a Cambodian rice paddy with a U.S. Marine captain riding on my back. I'm telling you true, it was him. Older, but it was him. I was just about ready to follow him, figured I'd violate all my principles and do some personal work, take him down on a side street, when this green sedan stops and my real target gets out.

"This is all happening in the space of seconds, understand, so I had some quick choices to make. I went for the whole bundle, both of 'em. Outside the window in El Niño there's a pole with a guywire attached to it. My effective field of fire was only about four feet between the wire and the pole. It was tricky, particularly with a handgun, but not *that* tricky. Since the navy man was walking and would have been out of my sight in a second, I pulled down on him first, went for a chest shot, but I was a little high and hit him in the neck, I think. I was using magnum hollowpoints, though, so it probably worked out if medical attention was slow in coming. It shouldn't have taken two shots on the civilian. Like I said before, feeling a little slippage in my skills, or my attitude, maybe both.

185

"As I see it now, shooting the navy man was a mistake, at least in the time and place I picked. The basic rule in this business is never let your own personal feelings get tangled up with your work and never do a hit for personal reasons, period. That's how you get in trouble, you can be connected in some way to the hit. You probably don't know this, but most professional killers are never even suspected of having done a job, let alone caught. The idea is to remain unobtrusive, and I broke that rule in Puerto Vallarta. Lost control because of something personal that happened years ago. It's in my file somewhere . . . well known I'd sworn to kill that navy bastard if I ever found him. I was warned, about ten years ago, not to even think about it, that he was in some special branch of the navy hooked up with the CIA . . . something important and undeniably mean."

"What happened after the helicopter took off and left you standing there in a Cambodian rice paddy?"

"You don't want to know in any detail or you'll never be able to eat again. The captain and I were tortured." The shooter held out his hands, and Danny saw deep scars around the fingernails he hadn't noticed before. He pointed to the missing finger on his left hand. "They sawed this off with a

186

rusty jungle knife, just as a warm-up for the really bad stuff. The captain died from what they did to us. I killed a guard, garroted him with a piece of wire one night, and escaped. Came to a river and floated down it on logs until I came to the sea. Worked my way southeast along the Gulf of Thailand, living off the land and friendly villagers until I ran into an army patrol three weeks later. I tell you, I looked all over 'Nam for that bastard who left me standing in the rice paddy with the captain slung over my back, but he'd apparently been rotated out and was gone."

Luz came back just as the shooter was finishing his story. Later on Danny would tell her all of what the shooter had said.

"I don't quite know how to say this, but how do you live with it . . . with the things you've been talking about?"

"You mean how do I live with the killing?"

"Yeah, that. You're five and oh in the last few days."

Clayton Price smiled. "First off, after 'Nam I stopped keeping score; just do the work now, and there's no such thing as a losing record in this business, anyway. Beyond that, depends on how you see morality or whatever it's called. Westerners, Americans in particular, are a bunch of hypocrites when it comes to killing. Other day I read about seventeen babies being born with empty brain cavities up in the Brownsville hospital, supposedly due to industrial pollution. The article talked about all kinds of sewage and toxic waste running down the gutters, clouds of shit drifting over the workers' shacks. Most of it coming from American factories located over there to avoid U.S. environmental laws and wage levels.

"In my mind, there's no qualitative difference between those business executives and me. Well, maybe one — my killing's surgical, theirs is indiscriminate. Hell, it just goes on and on, all over the place. If it isn't a gun, it's pollution. If it isn't either of those or cars with exploding gas tanks or about a million other things, gravity eventually takes us all down. Think about the American Indians, how we wiped 'em out. Then think about trumped-up wars in far-off places. When I get down real tight on it, see it straight and clean, I know I killed two or three hundred people in Southeast Asia for no other reason than to satisfy the egos of politicians and generals. I was a mercenary there, too, only I was too young to realize it. One way or the other, economics or religion lies at the bottom of it.

"Savings-and-loan executives running off

with money and driving old people to despair and emotional wreckage. Young Eskimos machine-gunning walruses so tusks can be swapped for drugs. The Crusades, the IRA, the lynching of blacks, the Holocaust, the Conquistadors — we're all in the killing business, one way or the other. You probably buy products made in those Matamoros factories, making you an accessory, and claims of not knowing it's going on don't wash, 'cause you know it's going on.

"Look, I'm tired and ranting a bit. I came to terms with what I do a long time ago. I just do it and don't try to justify it. But I saw your face twitching when I was telling you about shooting that VC woman while she was peeing, and I can get pretty goddamn hot about that kind of naiveté. Americans think the rest of the world views life the way middle-class Presbyterians do. That's horseshit. There's lots of ways of viewing life. We point to the Ten Commandments and say human life is sacred, put here to serve God and all that, keeps the troops in line. Others thump on Hindu scripture and say this life is nothing more than a stage on the way to something else. The VC didn't seem to think much about killing or dying or cutting the nuts off American pilots. Or how about the L.A. gangs? They're just like Charlie. Life means nothing to them, a perfectly flat value structure when it comes to killing. Sometime, maybe I'll tell you about the plan certain high-placed government officials had to send me into L.A. and clean up things a bit, take out the main honchos. Never came off, but they had the idea, and I was thinking about doing it.

"I remember your book, Danny, *Chicago Underground* . . . when'd it come out? Six, seven years ago? I knew I'd seen your face somewhere before, but it took me a while to put it together with a photo on the dust jacket of a book I'd read."

"Yeah, it came out in 1987." Danny was on the run.

"So you hung around with the wiseguys for a while and think you got the inside dope. Ever see one of 'em do a hit?"

"No."

"For chrissake, you think you got hold of what really happens and put it down on paper, a few spicy little tales of life on the dark side, a few limp inferences about the way you think things operate." The shooter moved his head in derision, coming into full spate now. "You missed hearing the sound of a man's kneecaps splintering when they're whacked with a tire iron. You missed the thirty-eight slug in some guy's head and more thirty-eight slugs in his wife's chest because she happened to witness the whole thing. Ever see up close what a bullet does to the insides of a human being, how it goes in small, cutting what's called a permanent wound channel and then maybe starts bouncing around off the ribs and sternum and spine, like a missile ricocheting around inside Madison Square Garden? If it's a hollow-point bullet, it goes in small and fragments inside, steel slivers flying off and slicing into organs every which way. Danny Pastor, Chicago tough guy and street-smart journalist, you haven't seen anything, you just think you have. You and the rest of the goddamn phonies watching *Murder, She Wrote*, where the killing takes place off stage, safe and clean, real polite. I love those murder mystery weekends they have at hotels, where everybody pecks around trying to figure out who killed some distant character. I can tell you that if they came snooping around the people in my business, they'd get their insides gouged out by icepicks or worse. The problem is we've cheapened the idea of killing, so it's everyman's intellectual game, except a few of us actually do it and know what killing means, and it's an untidy business."

He'd moved over onto Danny's turf, just a little, when he'd mentioned the wiseguys.

Danny was feeling puny and embarrassed because he knew the shooter was at least partly right about what he was saying and wanted to get on another track. "Any of your work ever involve the mob?"

"A little, not much. They stay in the cities mostly, and I don't have an edge there. They're pretty shrewd and smart on the concrete. I don't have a good feel for cities. But in open country they are soft boys and they are mine." He said it pure and simple, no self-aggrandizement, just the straight of it all.

"Piss on it." Clayton Price stood up. "I've had it, got to get some rest. What about the Bronco?"

"I'll look at it tomorrow, first light. Sounded like something serious."

"What then?"

"I don't know. Get a part for it in Mazatlán if I can. Maybe rent a car down there."

"We'll talk about it at first light. If I don't sleep I'm going to fall over right here." He started to walk away, then turned. "You remember my little lecture back down the road, I hope. I sleep, you do what you have to. But think about the consequences before you do it."

"I remember."

He walked off, out of the cantina and across the little courtyard. Danny watched the swing of his right leg and thought about the Beretta riding there. The shooter: from the high frontiers of Pluto or somewhere else, who'd followed his own trace through the haze of distant autumns while he, Danny Pastor, had been boogeying down at the University of Missouri, supposedly studying journalism but spending most of his middle two years bouncing on the sweet, eager body of Missy Morganthal. Missy Morganthal, whose father ran an Indiana steel mill and gave lots of money to the UM athletic program. Missy Morganthal, a Kappa Kappa Gamma to Danny's Sigma Chi. Her tender, blond, ponytailed self perpetually hot and wet and right there for the taking. That is, until she'd hooked up with a young, McLuhan-esque media professor who had a neat apartment, talked her language, and offered something better than South Padre Island over spring break.

All of that, and out there on a parallel course of his own, the shooter had been coming along through the years. Like some specter, shaped by the dies of his genes and nurture or lack of it, bent on brutal tasks good people would rather not think about. And, if they did think about it, hoping someone else would do them. Danny knew Vietnam had been a blue-collar war, fought by the working class and citizens of color. Fought by young men like the shooter, who went because they were told to go and were scorned afterward by those who didn't go and would never understand what had really happened there. At that moment, Danny Pastor didn't feel much like a hotshot journalist who'd set out on this trip with the intent of recapturing old glories. He felt . . . childlike, and guilty in a way he couldn't articulate to himself.

Somewhere down the night streets of Zapata, dogs were snarling. Danny took a last swallow of the beer he'd been holding and looked over at Luz. She was staring toward the door and into the courtyard where the shooter had gone.

She turned to Danny and touched his face. "Danny, I need you to make love to me."

They went to their room and did that, in a quiet, subdued way, looking for some kind of something, safety maybe. And in the course of it, Luz María imagined she was being taken by a black horseman the old people used to talk about, an avenging spirit who rode only on the darkest nights and took people away without warning, especially young women.

Later that night, Danny awakened and sat by the window, thinking, looking for a way out of the mess. He sat there for a long time. It was around three o'clock, the village sleeping, Western Hemisphere sleeping. Something moved in the shadows, staying close to a row of buildings down the street. A big dog, probably, but then it came under a street lamp for a moment: a jaguar, *el tigre*. The cat walked Zapata's streets like a low-slung, rosetted nightwatchman, head swinging from side to side, big paws moving over the cobblestones. Danny's chair squeaked when he shifted to get a better look. From thirty feet away *el tigre* looked up at the window where he was sitting, stared at him for ten seconds, yellow green eyes Danny could see even in poor light. The jaguar turned a corner, still walking slowly, and moved up a dark side street out of sight. A minute or two later, Danny heard the death squeal of something, dog or pig or burro. The sound lasted for only an instant.

Danny returned to bed and lay there. In the stillness, he heard the scratch of a key at the door next to his. After that, a soft click as the shooter's door opened and swung shut again.

Soft click of one door in a mountain village called Zapata, and the slam of another on a red Chevy Suburban parked behind a Pemex station south of Mazatlán.

Walter McGrane, sweaty and jowled,

leaned against the car door he'd just shut and kicked at the dust. "Goddamn it all, didn't we specifically tell 'em all not to shit around with Clayton Price? We've got to get it through their thick, wetback heads this ain't no drunken tourist or small-time heist man we're dealing with."

A Mexican polka was roaring out of the *federale* truck next to him. "Turn that goddamn radio off, let me think!"

The radio went dead, and Walter McGrane squinted up at the mercury vapor lights above him. Two men in windbreakers stood nearby.

One of them asked, "Think this is Price's work?"

Walter McGrane growled back, "Hell, yes. Who else?" He whacked the rear door of the Suburban. "That mess in there has his signature all over it, precision shooting, small-bore handgun. Their weapons haven't even been fired, they never got a round off. But stashing the truck here was sloppy; I'd have expected better of Price. He's obviously in a hurry. . . . Jesus, it smells bad in there.

"Weatherford" — he looked at one of the men with him — "get on the wire and tell 'em we're going to concentrate on the Mazatlán area. Get some supporting firepower up here and some trench workers to start scouring the countryside. Tell 'em I want

196

everybody here by early morning."

Walter McGrane went into the station for coffee, decided he needed to make water, and stood at the urinal, wishing he were back in Georgetown. If it hadn't been for the fiasco last year in South Yemen, which wasn't his fault to begin with as he saw it, he probably wouldn't even be here.

"This is a chance to redeem yourself, Walter." They'd told him that at the briefing.

Screw redemption. He'd do this one right because he'd been ordered to do it. After it was over, he'd retire and move to his little farm in Vermont, raise apples and sit quiet on the front porch, try not to stare overmuch at the young minister's wife when she came by for bridge on Thursday evenings.

THE ROSARY AND
CLAYTON PRICE

Early morning, Friday. Danny under the
Bronco's hood, shooter looking on. Roosters
making one hell of a racket all over the village,
burros hungry and screeching. Music from
a tape deck down the street, Mexican stuff,
accordion and guitars and love songs.

Danny straightened up and leaned on Vito's
fender, staring down at the engine. "Broken
fuel pump."

"Can we get a new one anywhere around
here?"

"Maybe. Possibly in Mazatlán . . . probably. There's a number of these old geezers
in Mexico. Might have to go to a junkyard
and find a replacement. It'll take time . . .
a day, maybe more. I could rent a car instead."

Clayton Price shook his head. "That won't
do. Rental cars leave a paper trail. They'll
need your driver's license and so on. I don't
know where this is all heading and whether

you'll even be able to return the car or not. In that case, we'll have cops looking for a stolen rental car, and they'll have your driver's license and address. No good. Can you fix the Bronco if you find a fuel pump?"

"I think so."

"How far are we from the border?"

"Twenty hours' driving time . . . twenty *hard* hours." Danny was leaning against a fender, arms folded.

"It always comes down to crap like this, crucified on a fuel-pump cross or some other screwup." Clayton Price jammed both hands in his pockets and looked up at the church steeple a block away as the bells began to toll for Friday mass. "Did a job in Africa once, me and another guy. Way back in the bush. Nice clean piece of work, and we were running for Kenya when a fan belt broke, and no spare. Can you imagine that, no spare fan belt for a job that had heavy financing?"

"What happened?"

It was the first time Danny had ever seen the shooter actually laugh. "While we were standing around on this dirt track in the middle of absolute, bloody nowhere Africa, two Land Rovers came by, a photo expedition for tourists. They picked us up, and I rode for six hours beside some guy from Ohio who told me everything there was to know about his paper box business in Cleveland. My spotter, a Chicano guy named Juliano, from East L.A., ended up running off to Cairo with one of the women on the expedition. I stayed at a fancy safari lodge for three days until I caught a ride to Nairobi. All this time, half the incompetents from something called the Varagunzi Revolutionary Front were stampeding all over central Africa looking for us. Jesus, it was . . . what's the word? . . . surreal. Three months later I heard Juliano had contracted some kind of intestinal parasite in Cairo and died from it after this woman had set him up in Dallas as her gigolo. He sent me a picture of himself sitting on a condo balcony, in a white bathrobe and smoking a cigar."

Clayton Price kicked a small rock with the toe of his desert boot. "Shit. As Juliano used to say, when things go bad, they really go bad. All right, get on into Mazatlán. Luz and I'll stay here."

Danny figured he knew what the shooter was thinking and how he was thinking. He was gambling Danny wouldn't go looking for serious law if Luz was still back in the village with him. He was right, mostly. The thought about getting himself out of this and saying to hell with everyone else had already twinkled through his mind during the night. Luz

200

might be his little darlin' at the moment, but he'd been picking up on something over the last few months, that Luz might have her own agenda she hadn't been sharing with him. He'd felt it back in Puerto Vallarta and had been feeling it even more during this wild ride through Mexico, something to do with endings, as if an idea called "Luz & Danny" was curling up like a brown leaf in the Kansas autumns of his boyhood. Still, he couldn't do that to her, pull out and leave her stranded in a place called Zapata with a prince of darkness.

An old funky green vehicle of the school bus variety came through the village at noon with Mazatlán whitewashed on its windshield. Below that were listed the villages where it stopped, going and coming, including Zapata. Luz and the shooter walked with Danny to where he caught the bus, broken fuel pump under his arm in a brown paper bag. He looked out the window at them as the bus turned around and headed out of the village, bending along the cobblestone streets, groaning and lurching toward Mazatlán. And it struck him at that moment, seeing the two of them standing side by side, that Luz somehow looked like she belonged more to the shooter than to him, if she belonged to anybody at all.

201

Down through the Sierra Madre foothills and into the flat country again. Past the villages, past the dogs maundering around or sleeping in the dirt. The yellow-brown dogs, sores and sad eyes, long legs and long noses. Must be a breed called Mexican village dog. At the inspection station east of Concordia the bus was waved through. Same five men standing there in almost the identical positions where they'd been the previous evening, like a tableau plunked down in the Mexican countryside.

In Concordia things looked more ominous. A black-and-white patrol car was parked along the road, two Dodge pickups and two black Suburbans next to it. Also a police bus and a white Dodge van. *Federales,* police, and three gringos, talking. All of them heavily armed.

Danny's bus was halted for a moment while a truckload of soldiers pulled across the highway and stopped near the other vehicles. An older gringo, in a sweat-stained safari jacket and holding a bullhorn, climbed on the hood of a truck and began talking to the others. Below him, another gringo in a windbreaker was translating the other man's words into Spanish.

Danny couldn't make out what was being said. He was thinking of the thin, gray-haired man and the young, soft Mexican woman back in Zapata. A goddamned invasion force was being assembled and it'd be coming into the mountain villages and it'd eventually get to Zapata, sometime . . . or sooner. Maybe before he returned with a fuel pump for a twenty-five-year-old Bronco. The differential gear in the bus sounded like a pistol hammer being slowly drawn back as it rolled west toward Mazatlán, under the great bend of what more and more looked to Danny like a hostile cosmos.

Danny had passed through Mazatlán several years back and had no sense of the place other than it was big and full of tourism and shipping and heavy industry. But he had a plan. The rental car agencies supplied off-road vehicles of various stripes so tourists could drive out and ruin the beaches. He took a taxi to a Hertz office in the hotel district and asked where they got their jeeps and so forth repaired, saying he needed an engine part. The nice young Mexican woman at the counter told him, and he taxied over there.

The mechanic looked at the fuel pump and shook his head, *no bomba de gasolina* — he didn't have one, from what Danny could make out. They floundered around in two different languages and got confused. A man standing nearby came over and asked if he could help. He interpreted: The fuel pump was for a very old model and only junkyards might have one, what Danny had already guessed. Danny was given directions to a large salvage place and got back in his taxi. By the time he'd located the junkyard, it had closed for the day.

The taxi dropped him off at the Hotel Belmar, one of Mazatlán's original inns. Fine old building with painted tiles, dark woods, and bullfight posters pasted on the walls. When night came he walked north along the sea and into the south end of the main tourist district. American kids everywhere, behaving like assholes. He turned around and eventually found a small restaurant near the hotel. The fish soup was good, and he lingered there for a long time over coffee.

On the way back to the hotel he picked up an English-language newspaper. The article was on page one: KILLER SOUGHT IN NATIONWIDE MANHUNT. It reported much of what he already knew and went on to say

One of the victims, George Cooper, was formerly a computer engineer with Frontier Science, Inc., in Dallas, Texas. The second victim, Captain L. K. Reece, United States Navy, received a fatal wound in the neck. Both shootings are believed to be the work of a professional assassin. According to an unidentified source in the United States, the killer is a former Marine Corps sergeant who was well known in the Vietnam conflict for his deadly accuracy with all types of weapons and for his merciless approach to killing. The source described him as "thorough and unrelenting when he takes an assignment. He is deadly, a man without normal human feelings who will kill without mercy and who cares for nothing except his own survival and the task at hand." The source refused to identify the suspect by name and further declined to say why this particular man is the suspect. Mexican authorities originally tried to suppress all news of the incident, but now have stated the suspect is heavily armed and should be considered extremely dangerous. All branches of the Mexican police as well as the Mexican army and representatives from U.S. law enforcement agencies are cooperating in the manhunt.

The children of Zapata toward sundown, skipping along the street and singing an old rhyme from the Mexican equivalent of *Mother*

Goose: "Just as the sun was coming up/The night before today/A blind man sat writing down/What a deaf-mute had to say."

The women of Zapata toward sundown: "Hail Mary, full of grace, the Lord is with Thee . . ." The rosary. And in ragged unison it drifted through the open church door and reached almost to the plaza but failed to make it quite that far on the evening air. If more had come to pray, the appeals for Mary to intercede with her son Jesus on their behalf might have reached farther, but only seven women knelt there about halfway up the center aisle.

Clayton Price stood in the side entrance to the church and watched the women and listened to them and to Luz María, who had no beads to count but had joined the women anyway after borrowing for her head his blue bandanna with white half-moon decorations on it. The women had already glanced at her and the gringo and gone on praying while Luz María looked over her shoulder once, then once again at the tall, thin man backlighted in the church door. Clayton Price could feel the sun's heat on his shoulders even then when it was low. Inside the church's thick adobe walls the air was cooler and smelled heavily of oils and incense and sins that had been forgiven long before the ending of this day in the Mexican cordillera, long before Clayton Price ever held a gun in his hands.

The family of Clayton Price was not religious, but he had prayed once . . . prayed that he be allowed to die and doing that more with his mind than with his voice, for he hadn't been able to get any words on his tongue at the very moment when he'd been naked and tied to a bamboo frame, and was being tortured in ways so hideous he'd eventually sent the memories of them to a place where they lay quiet and could not be resurrected unless he consciously chose to bring them back. The scars on his body were restless and tried to make him remember, but they could not, and he had a way of making his eyes go peculiar and unfocused so the scars weren't visible in any mirrors he might stand before.

He listened to the women's voices and paid attention to little movements inside of him as he did, something he wanted to feel, while at the same time disliking the sense of being fragile that seemed to come directly from those feelings. He listened and watched the woman Luz María, thinking of her as she had bathed yesterday in the stream. He'd seen at that time the smooth brown skin and vertebrae standing out against it when she'd bent forward and the breast she'd shown for only a quick moment and smiling as she'd done it. And he remembered just how her body had looked to him and the old things buried deep but coming forward when he'd seen her like that.

If he had not found that length of wire in the dirt of a Cambodian hut and used it as he had the night he'd escaped and on the way out almost severing the neck of a man who had tortured him, he might never have had those feelings again. For the little men in black had pricked his anal area with sharp bamboo and waved knives around him and pointed them at his testicles, saying "tomorrow" in his language and making a noise with their voices sounding like the cut of a knife itself and laughing when they'd said it.

There had been some of that in what had happened yesterday at the beach restaurant in Teacapán when the hombres were laughing at him. The same twisted faces, the same mean smiles saying, "We will do things to you later." He'd learned over his life to back out of those situations when nothing was at stake and let them go by and walk away, sometimes hearing laughter saying he was a coward or worse. In his business you did not draw attention either to yourself or your skills.

But the old jungle memories and the instinct to survive were only part of why he'd done what he'd done under the thatched roof by the sea in Teacapán. The woman Luz María had been part of it, too, and he hadn't liked being taunted that way in front of her and wasn't sure now whether he was only being protective as a father might have been or, on the other hand, being prideful and shielding in the way of all men who rise to fight for a woman they wish to have for their own. He'd lied to Danny when he'd said all eight hombres coming at once would have made a difference in the way things turned out. A *little* difference maybe, and he would have suffered more than a scrape on his face, but he could have killed them all with his hands and knife and beer bottles and their own machetes turned back on them, or with the Beretta if things had gotten real disorderly. The man with a broken nose and shattered cheekbone had come away lucky; Clayton Price could have taken the man's eyes just as easily as he broke the cheekbone and the nose on the face above the body where a machete swung.

And standing there while the rosary sounded, he remembered his private oath taken over thirty years ago that he would never care again, never expose himself to all the hurt caring brought. But the woman Luz María was kneeling before a god Clayton Price didn't understand and had knelt over her parents' graves yesterday and prayed then, and was praying again here. And in a way he could not grasp, her prayers seem valid to him and should be answered, if this god she prayed to had any favors left to give after all He'd been asked for.

When the rosary was finished and the other women gone, Luz sat with him in a front pew and tried to explain Catholicism, how it had a comforting, nurturing side to it, in spite of the pope's insistence on women having as many babies as possible in a country where there were already too many babies riding on the hips of sixteen-year-old girls. The shooter didn't know much about Catholics, but he'd met a Jesuit priest once in Venezuela and drunk some wine with him. Luz said that didn't really count, since the Jesuits went their own way most of the time, almost like a separate religion all their own. Her mother had said as much after a Jesuit had come to their village seeking money for his foreign mission one time and gone off pretty much empty-handed but understanding also the people of Ceylaya didn't have much themselves.

Clayton Price told her what the Jesuit had

said: "You don't preach religion to people with hungry bellies. First you fill the bellies, then you preach religion."

Luz replied that sounded right to her, but that a lot of Mexican village priests had never quite grasped the idea. Mostly they prattled on about trusting in the Lord and not practicing birth control, though their attitudes had been discreetly changing in the last twenty years. The pope had come to Mexico once, in an effort to renew their fervor, and the priests had listened to him, but the pope didn't have to deal with women in the confessional who already had six children and couldn't adequately provide for them. When the pope left, the priests returned to searching for a fine line between the church's ideals and the practicality needed if their flocks were going to remain manageable.

Luz and the shooter left the church an hour before sunset. They walked through the winding paths of the village, past houses set into hillsides. The sound of mariachis came out of windows and doorways, radios filling the night with the sound of an older Mexico, one that was passing and would never come again. With the music behind them, they followed an old road down to the abandoned silver mines that had once made Zapata a place of treasure for the Spaniards and other

Europeans later on. The silver was taken out by mule, each mule carrying two 50-kilo ingots on its way to the sea. Most of the old mining machinery was gone, the Japanese having bought it just before the Second World War. They had come here and hauled the scrap to Mazatlán, shipped it to Japan, and melted it down for the metal.

Some of the mine entrances were still open, and Clayton Price wanted to go inside, but Luz thought it would be dangerous. He did it anyway while she waited outside. They walked back to the plaza by a different route from the one they'd taken, passing by a house where a young man was cutting an old man's hair in the twilight. The old man sat very still, the younger one talking softly and scissors moving.

There was only one telephone in the village, in a store near the church. The shooter gave the proprietor money to let him use the phone and made a collect call somewhere. Luz couldn't hear what he was saying, except for something that sounded like "Tortoise" and then the phrase "LC, silver mine," which he repeated several times. But she could tell he was angry, and he finished by nearly shouting, "Goddammit, you *owe* me this!" He slammed the phone down, then softened when he looked at her, and they went back to the cantina.

Earlier this day, after Danny Pastor had left for Mazatlán, Luz María and the shooter had taken a late lunch, sitting in the shade of the cantina's porch. She'd drunk a margarita and he'd drunk a beer.

She'd pointed toward the steep hillsides where village men were working. "They say in these hills a man can be killed by falling out of his cornfield."

And Clayton Price had laughed at that, the machete cut on his cheek hurting only a little when he'd crinkled his face. There were many ways to be killed; falling out of a cornfield was probably the better of most, though not a way men would choose to die, he'd thought. He'd watched her mouth as she'd spoken and wondered for a moment what it would be like to touch her and wanted to do it right then, except she'd turned and looked back at him with black female eyes appearing as if they might not mind if he did touch her, causing him to pull back. So he'd reached for his beer, looking up at the hillsides again, and pretended he was still smiling at what she had said about farmers tumbling out of their fields.

From the cantina's porch, he'd pointed to a house snuggled into the hills about a mile out and had said he wouldn't mind living there, living a quiet peasant's life. His eyes had gone lambent, and he'd said he sometimes wished he were five years old again and had the long carpet of innocence before him. That he felt like a lone, wild bird circling the ponds of autumn, looking for a place to land. That he regretted there'd been no Sunday afternoons in the park with children. Or softball games in the evenings, or a wedding in which he'd given the hand of his only daughter. None of that. No quiet rocking on a southern porch at sundown, gin and tonic in hand and savoring a day's work well done and in which no harm was intended or accomplished.

He'd told her of a recurring dream in the nights of his life. That he flew from a high trapeze, somersaulting through the air, but the bar where the catcher was supposed to be waiting was always empty. The dream never failed to end the same: he would slam onto the sawdust floor and lie there broken and dying, the audience applauding as it filed from the circus tent.

Luz had told him again how she wanted to live in the United States, that she'd do just about anything to get to *el Norte* and have the good things she'd seen on television. He'd asked why Danny didn't marry her and take her there. And she'd told him Danny had no interest in marrying her or anyone else and heading north with a woman on his arm.

Clayton Price wasn't dumb. It was his business to know something about human behavior. And he knew any sustained dance such as the one Luz and Danny had been doing for two years required mutual parasitism, a rough balance of gain and loss by both partners. So it wasn't merely a case of an alienated and heartless gringo getting what he could from a young Mexican woman. Wasn't Danny supporting both of them, and wasn't she living with him and dancing around the tables in Mamma Mia some nights and therefore getting something out of the deal?

He'd asked her what she knew about the United States. Did she really understand how she'd be treated up there if she was on her own? For that matter, how she'd be treated even if she was hanging out with a gringo and supposing even that gringo had pulled himself together and was making all the education and abilities he had pay off in American *dinero?*

She'd thought she understood and tried to explain what she'd do. But he'd said she'd either have to be well funded so she could tell everyone who didn't like her accent and skin color to go to hell or she'd have to develop a psyche capable of withstanding the kinds of attitudes she'd confront, in some parts of the country more than others. Luz had said that wouldn't be any problem, that she could handle whatever came up. But she was more than a little naive, and Clayton Price knew it. Still, he'd felt sorry for her, felt that and something more he couldn't quite lay his mind on at that time, sitting on the cantina porch and talking with her and seeing her all black eyed and female.

So he'd told her about his place in northern Minnesota, way back in the woods and near the Canadian border, not so far from the town of Grand Marais, lying there quiet next to the cold water where the big ore boats used to run. She could come and stay there if she wanted, if that's what she really wanted, and he had ways of getting her through the tangle up at Laredo or Nogales or wherever they had to make the border crossing. He lived there most of the time, in that northern land, that's what he said. What he didn't say was that he might not ever be able to go back there now, even though he picked up his mail at a town a hundred miles away as a way of protecting the secrecy of his home place. The hunters were smart; they'd find him.

He had another place, something he'd come across during one of his R&R excursions while he was in the military. On an island off Phuket, five hundred miles south of Bangkok. It was a bungalow on the beach. Paradise, he called it, and described the easy life you could live there. Luz didn't know where Thailand was, let alone Bangkok, let alone Phuket, but it had sounded wonderful to her.

He'd looked straight at her and warming to his own words and the way she was looking back at him, and started saying things about the Minnesota cabin in summer along with Phuket in winter. And that had sounded even better to Luz, who'd sat there hearing in her head the whine of big jet engines. And seeing herself paddling through cool northern waters during the summer heat and then wearing flowers in her hair and doing rhumbas on white sand in a far place called Phuket, somewhere south of another place called Bangkok she'd never seen on a map or even heard about at any time in her life. For a woman who'd crawled up out of a small, dusty village named Ceylaya, that wouldn't be too bad, and she'd leave those village hombres, who'd wanted to put her flat on her back and give her babies when she was fifteen, far gone and choking on her dust. And later on saying the rosary and looking over her shoulder at the gringo standing in the church doorway, she'd thought some more about cool lake water and warm Asian sand and had asked Mary the Virgin to intercede on her behalf and help take her to those places.

After the rosary and the walk to the silver mines, she sat on the cantina porch again with this man who had called himself Peter Schumann before but who now told her that really wasn't true and that his name was Clayton Price. She asked him more things about his cabin in the woods and would she need a heavy shawl when the hard weather came and what direction an airplane would go if it were heading for Phuket.

At the same evening moment as he smiled and told her more than a heavy shawl would be needed, a collective and appreciative moan rose from a group of hombres standing near the cantina. From behind adobe houses and sashaying up the cobblestones out of the east section of the village was a señorita of maybe fourteen and wearing snug faded jeans rolled to her knees and black shoes and even socks that were black also. She was beautiful in the face and just as fine in the body and knew exactly what she had and, unlike Luz María at that age, was not afraid of giving promise to the hombres who continued with their murmurs of approval just loud enough for the señorita to hear.

The hombres then began making another sound that was kind of low and wet as she smiled at the heavens and passed by. All of them with their eyes followed the swing of her backside as she went to the plaza and sat there with two boys of her own age who were wishing they had enough money to play the Nintendo game at the store near the church. And the men near the cantina still watched her, the young ones uncommitted and searching and also the older ones, who were considering the possibilities of what might come along after she'd had a baby or two by one of their amigos and maybe would start looking for a little variety beyond the range of her husband. And also hoping all the while some rich gringo wouldn't come drifting through here and see the possibilities himself, offering her for a week or two more than a village man could hope to offer in a lifetime. Maybe offering a trip to the white sands of southern Thailand, maybe that or other things of equal value.

But village girls with dreams beyond sweeping dirt floors for a lifetime and sustaining a weekly beating from a husband just for good measure, him doing that merely to show who's boss in the family, have to do what's necessary. So Luz knew she, herself, was being manipulative and yet at the same time felt genuine things warm and female toward this man, Clayton Price.

He was talking to her and opening up in the way men have sometimes of talking to women and saying all the things they never say to other men. "I used to feel in control of things, like nothing could touch me if I used my head and played it smart. In the last few years I've started to feel vulnerable. Not sure why . . . age, maybe, maybe age does that to you. You start looking back and see you're going to leave nothing behind other than a trail of bodies in the jungles and alleyways of the world. Not sorry for what I've done, but I've got some regrets about what I haven't done. I would have liked to have a wife and children, now that I think about it, but there was no way I could do what I do and be married. It just wouldn't have worked, would it? Can't you just hear it: 'My daddy sells insurance, what does your daddy do?' 'Oh, my daddy's a sniper; he shoots people in the back from long distances.' "

Luz reached out and took his hand when he said that and thought she could see a little hint of tears in his eyes. But whatever was there dried up fast. He talked on and on about his life, about his boyhood in Brooklyn when he'd wanted to be a mountain man or a pitcher for the old Brooklyn Dodgers, about going out to Minnesota later on. The wound on his face was crusted over and still looked angry. Luz felt deeply sorry for him in some ways and oddly loving toward him in other ways. And something else there was about him that made her both sexually excited and feeling almost submissive, as if he were in control of her and as if she had no choice but to stay with him here or go where he said they should go.

He spoke to her. "Standing there in the church, listening to you and the others say the rosary, something started to work on my insides. I've always thought of myself as hard and untouchable — the marines had a lot to do with it; you had to believe that about yourself to go off into the jungle for a week and lie there in the grass and kill people — but there was something about the women's voices, and the church, and how you looked with my bandanna tied around your head. For a moment there I was wishing I'd lived my life as a simple farmer, like the men in Zapata who come in from the fields every day and sit on their front steps talking with one another after supper."

He'd drunk three beers by this time, and Luz had drunk with him, bottle for bottle, both of them talking and yet watching the teenage lovers around the plaza who came to the benches every night about this hour. Later, after they had eaten white tortillas with slivers of *cabrito* and salsa, they walked across the courtyard toward their rooms. Luz took hold of Clayton Price's hand and was surprised at how strong it felt, stronger than she'd thought it would feel since his hands seemed pretty thin just lying on a cantina table. She stopped and looked up at him, the string of colored lights above them. Some lights on, some off, one flickering.

There was no one in the courtyard to see her stand on her tiptoes and pull the face of Clayton Price toward her, kissing him soft and long and then moving her hands to open his shirt and touch the hair and skin on his chest. He was awkward but kissed her back and touched her hair and stroked it and held it in both his hands, and he did that for a long time as if he'd never touched a woman's hair before.

When they came to his room, he unlocked the door and Luz went inside with him. She undressed him and then herself and lay beside him. He was white and angular and less threatening with his clothes off, not seeming as tall and powerful to her. She touched him, and he touched her in a tentative way. She took his right hand and laid it on her breast, thinking all the while of the weapons he'd held in that hand, the index finger pulling triggers, the thumb drawing hammers back. His thumb had a callus on it, and it excited her in a strange way to think that hand was touching her breast.

And though she did her best, talking soft to him and touching him in all the right places with her hands and mouth, running her fingers along the length of his scars, some of which started on his thighs and moved directly up to his manhood, the shooter was unable to come erect and make love to her. She wanted him to do that, wanted it in the worst way, wanted in some curious fashion to experience making love to a man who could do what he could do with a gun in his hand and make others fall before his strength and skill. She was wet and high sexed, wanting him and feeling sorry for him and feeling controlled by him all at the same time, a woman-mother-child rolled into one.

But there were parts of him so long neglected, and these being of both mind and body, that even when opportunity and some kind of fluttering desire were there, the whole of them remained less than the necessary sum and were overwhelmed by the prospect. He couldn't get hard and rolled over on his back and looked at the ceiling for a long time, then said he wanted to sleep. Luz touched his chest and put her arms around him, sleeping there beside him. When she awakened on Saturday morning, he was gone. She dressed and went outside. He was sitting on a bench in the plaza, looking at the old church, while a woman with a shovel and plastic bag moved around the plaza, yelling, "*Vamos!*" at wandering pigs and scooping animal dung from the cobblestones.

And during this time Danny was gone, Luz saw two other things. She'd watched Clayton Price clean the Beretta and said to Danny later on how he'd handled it sure and easy with a quick, light touch. He'd also repacked his knapsack, getting it ready, she supposed, in case they had to get out of Zapata fast. Danny asked her about the gun he'd seen him put in there after he did the shooting in Puerto Vallarta. Luz said there was no gun in the knapsack. So Danny figured the shooter didn't want to be caught carrying the weapon and must have thrown it away or hidden it in the Bronco. He'd searched the Bronco, but the gun wasn't there. He asked what else she'd found out, and she said the man's real name was Clayton Price.

MONDAYS NEVER COME

The salvage yard owner was impatient. It was Saturday and a Mexican version of Mother's Day tomorrow when a fiesta celebrating the Madonna would be held. Danny was searching hard for a fuel pump, while the owner stayed close, haranguing him about getting out and coming back on Monday — *"Ándele, ándele."* Danny knew Monday would never come. Tuesday would, but not Monday. The hombre would be hung over from the fiesta and probably wouldn't even open up on "St. Monday," as it was called in Mexico.

"Un momentito, por favor, encontrar bomba de gasolina," Danny kept saying in badly pronounced Spanish, buying time, pawing through parts, climbing under the hoods of old Ford trucks, looking for anything that might work. At the far end of the yard, with bougainvillea growing around it, no less, was a crumpled cousin of Vito, rusting down and looking rougher even than Vito. But under the hood was a fuel pump in reasonably good condition, a little rusty, but looking okay

225

other than that. Danny bought it for two dollars, and, for another ten, picked up two five-gallon gas cans that'd strap on Vito's rear.

He took a taxi to the bus station and caught the last bus up to Zapata just as it pulled out. Two hours later, after stopping at most of the little villages along the way, he stepped down to Zapata's cobblestones and headed toward where he'd parked the Bronco, empty gas cans clanking as he walked.

Luz and the shooter were sitting in the shade of the cantina's porch and saw him coming. When they started down the street to meet him, Danny held up the brown paper bag and said, "Got it!"

It took Danny the rest of the afternoon to install the new pump. By the time he finished, he was hot and greasy and generally out of sorts. Luz and the shooter looked fresh after their baths and stood around watching while Danny swore and turned wrenches, finally getting it done and slamming the hood afterward. He started the engine, which still sounded rough and noisy but no worse than it ever had. The three of them took a trial spin around the village, then up on the highway. Fifteen minutes later they returned and Danny said the Bronco would take them onward to wherever the hell it was they were going.

Leave tomorrow morning, then?

No. Luz wanted to celebrate the Feast of the Madonna with the villagers, and the shooter had agreed to that.

"Are you serious?" Danny said, and then described what he'd seen at Concordia, a small army including gringo cops of some kind, and what the hell did the shooter think of that.

"I'm not surprised. I expected it."

"Do they know who you are?"

"Maybe. Depends on who's talked to whom. This operation's been a little too open right from the start."

"I mean, do they know what you look like?"

"Maybe. The military and other branches of the government have records, keep track of those people who've done work for them. Each of us in this business has a certain style — trademarks — no matter how much we try not to have them."

The shooter didn't say anything else except they'd lay low tomorrow and think about pulling out on Monday. Danny recalled what the shooter had said about the Las Noches crowd and their kamikaze lifestyles, and decided about then the shooter had joined them, maybe Luz as well, taking Danny Pastor along as an unwilling accomplice. Danny tried for a moment to think about death wishes but got overpowered by the concept and let it go.

They had dinner about nine o'clock, and Danny stumbled off to bed, so tired he had trouble going to sleep. Through the window he could see lightning farther back in the eastern mountains. Luz and the shooter were quietly talking somewhere outside, on the balcony. But he couldn't make out what they were saying. During the night, Danny awakened, chilly and almost shivering. He rolled over to snuggle up against Luz, but she wasn't there. He was too tired to think about it just then and went back to sleep.

Danny got up shortly after dawn. Luz's side of the bed was still empty, and he stood there contemplating the unwrinkled sheets for a few seconds, trying to figure out what lay in that emptiness. The wind came up, and a soft rain began falling through thin, yellow sunlight. The trees bent, and there was rain across the valleys, and he could see it falling upon the tile roofs and upon the dirt roads and the cobblestone streets of Zapata. And it ran down the tiles and onto the cobblestones and along the streets and moved downward toward the valleys in the way that water goes. Outside his window was a peacock tree, red blossoms wet and dripping. But the serious rains were still several weeks yet to come, and the shower degenerated into a slow drizzle after a few minutes.

By the time he was dressed, the wind and rain had gone completely, mist rising from the valleys. The cantina owner had shown them how to make their own coffee in case no one was tending things early in the morning, which there never was. The pot was half full and still passably warm. He poured a cup and strolled outside. People were already up and moving along the wet streets, carrying flowers and headed in the direction of the little cemetery on the northwest edge of the village. After a while the shooter and Luz came walking from that direction. They'd been up to the cemetery, where Luz had said a prayer for her own mother and both of them sheltering beneath a tree until the rain had passed.

Did Danny want to go to mass with them?

What? . . . Mass, for chrissake?

He could imagine the shooter kneeling down and making sure the Beretta didn't show when his pant leg hiked up. But they were serious, and Luz said later Clayton Price had taken off his gun and left it in his room when they went to mass.

Church bells on a Sunday morning, and the faithful gathered in front of the church, nodding and greeting each other before going inside. Danny sat on the cantina porch and drank coffee, visions of small armies assembling and moving all around them, road by road, village by village. Across the plaza he could see the shooter and Luz entering the church, Luz wearing a little straw hat with a black ribbon around the crown and a light yellow dress hemmed just above her knees. The hat had come from a store down the street. A village woman had made the dress for her, working all Saturday afternoon and into the evening to finish it since the shooter had promised double her normal price.

After a while Danny walked over to the main door of the church and looked in. The priest was holding up a chalice, saying words. The faithful said words back to him. Behind the priest was a huge cross. Crepuscular light slanted through stained-glass windows, coloring orange a suffering Jesus, hanging, crucified. Men die for a variety of reasons, their own or somebody else's.

Luz and the shooter were about halfway up on the right side, standing with the rest of the villagers. She reached out and hooked her arm around one of his. Jesus-on-the-cross-above-'em, Danny thought; they looked like the young lovers he'd seen lollygagging around the plaza in the blue, mountain evenings. And he tried again to think about just what the hell kinds of interpersonal transitions were happening and what the hell they were still hanging around Zapata for. And, most of all, why was Danny Pastor still hanging around? Fear, maybe. Something else, maybe. Maybe some kind of allegiance to Luz or, God help him, to Clayton Price and seeing through a bargain to the end.

When the mass ended, the priest stood at the church door with his acolytes and shook hands with the parishioners as they left. He smiled and spoke to Luz and the shooter. Danny watched him take the hand of Clayton Price and wondered if the slightest trace of cordite might linger on the priest's hand and if he would smell it later on.

The cantina owner had told Luz and the shooter about an old Spanish church outside of town, one of many places in Mexico called Guadalupe. A field trip had been planned for later that afternoon. Danny was wallowing in total disbelief by this time and began feeling more than a little mutinous. Mass . . . Luz and the shooter with arms joined . . . a field trip — this was dementia, "super-nuts," as he'd once heard an old physicist say in Las Noches. The physicist had been a member of the Los Alamos team that developed the first workable A-bomb.

Danny had never known what super-nuts felt like until that afternoon, driving out of Zapata on a field trip with the warriors of springtime surely closing in around them. All they needed was a wicker basket filled with picnic goodies and lemonade, but they didn't have one. Though, if Luz had thought about it ahead of time, the shooter would have found a wicker basket for her somewhere, maybe had it overnighted from L.L. Bean along with snorkeling equipment and rock-climbing gear.

The directions to this local Guadalupe were a little vague but workable: Go up on the highway, take the road to Ponuco when you see the sign, drive about six miles northeast along a dirt road hacked out of the mountainside — a road full of good-size rocks and barely wide enough for one vehicle — pull off the road when you come to a river, follow the river upstream on foot.

When they'd talked to the cantina owner and reconfirmed the directions to Guadalupe, Luz had overheard two hombres in the bar talking about all the soldiers in Concordia. They'd said a massive manhunt was going on all over Mexico for someone who had killed two men in Puerto Vallarta and that the bodies of three *federales* had been found at the Pemex station south of Mazatlán, so the search was being concentrated in this general area. She'd looked worried when she'd told the shooter and Danny what she'd heard. Danny was worried, too, but Clayton Price hadn't said anything, just chewed on his lower lip slightly while she talked.

It took them thirty minutes to work six miles back into the mountains. High up they went, thousand-foot drop-offs on the outer edge of the road. Vito climbed, and climbed more, then began a long descent into a deep valley where the river flowed. A Jeep, one of the flashy Baja models loaded with automotive trinkets and decorated with intricate striping, damn near ran them off the road on a blind curve. It looked expensive and new, with a long antenna waving from the rear of it and carrying four Mexican teenagers with bottles of beer in their hands.

"Pretty fancy Jeep," the shooter said. "How can someone in these villages afford something like that?"

"Drugs," Danny replied. "There's marijuana grown in commercial quantities all over the backcountry here. Lately the government's been carrying out one of its periodic crackdowns on drugs, so the dope growers have turned to robbery. That's the main reason for the increase in bandido activity along the main highways. The dope farmers have forgotten how to do any other kind of farming, or don't want to do it."

They reached the river and parked off the road on a dry portion of the riverbed. Luz still had on her yellow dress and hat, even though this was jeans-and-boots terrain. Her sandals were slippery on the river stones, so she took them off and hopped from flat rock to flat rock. Danny noticed how good her legs looked when she jumped from one rock to another, the yellow dress fluffing up.

They had to cross the river twice when it turned and cut them off at bluff outcroppings jutting out to the water's edge. The shooter and Danny crossed on rocks. Luz did the same on the first crossing. On the second the rocks were too far apart for her. The shooter walked back and picked her up, sloshing through the water while she held her sandals in one hand and laughed and wiggled her toes, the dress sliding high up to the tops of her thighs. Danny was starting to feel left out of things. It seemed Luz and the shooter were reaching an understanding at some pretty basic levels. Also, given the fact people were looking for them, there was some kind of psychological denial going on here, only Danny wasn't tuned in to it. They walked along a dirt path toward an old suspension bridge across the river, Luz humming and the shooter grinning like a schoolboy.

After thirty minutes of walking and jumping and finally crossing to the other side one more time via a dilapidated suspension bridge, they reached the old church. Though it was hard for Danny to concentrate, thinking as he was about the crunch they were in, he had to admit there was something special about wandering around the remains of a five-hundred-year-old Spanish church in the outback. The church had been built to serve a large mining operation, and the original flumes and sluices and stone structures where water wheels turned were still in place, made of river stone and looking capable of standing for another five hundred years. The roof on the church was gone, but the walls were still in place, and their voices echoed in there.

"Hola." The three of them swung around to see an old man coming into the church, dog with him. All of them said hello back to him. The old man said he was known as Don José Fierro and called himself the "Guardian of Guadalupe," a self-appointed position, Danny guessed. The old man was proud of his church and proud of his job, self-made though it was, showing them around and fetching an old newspaper clipping with a picture of him standing in the middle of the church. It had originally been

published in a Mazatlán tourist newspaper. He pointed out details of the place, took them on a tour of the entire area and then back to the church, where he showed them a statue of the Virgin of Guadalupe encased in plastic and hanging on a wall where the altar used to be.

They left twenty pesos with him and walked back toward the Bronco. Rounding a bend in the riverbed, they saw a man looking into the Bronco. The shooter went tight and into a half crouch, but Luz said it was only a curious farmer, and the tension eased. The farmer was embarrassed they'd caught him snooping, but Danny said, *"Buenas tardes,"* pleasantly, and the farmer seemed to feel a little better, waving and smiling as he drifted away.

Coming back into Zapata, the shooter instructed Danny to park the Bronco out of sight in a shallow arroyo behind where they were staying. Danny didn't ask why. They went to the cantina porch and sat there, evening drinks, evening talk.

The village hombres were getting an early start on the main fiesta celebration scheduled to begin at nine o'clock, two hours away. A couple of pickups were parked on the east side of the plaza, hoods lined with empty beer cans and the hombres lounging around the trucks. Suddenly a police car came up the street and turned into the plaza area.

"Stay put," the shooter said, watching the car. "If we move they'll notice it. Maybe they're just here to keep an eye on the boy-os, hold things in check on fiesta night."

The black-and-white moved slowly around the plaza, past the pickups. One of the hombres held out a beer to the cop on the passenger side, but the cop laughed and waved him off.

When they came around to where Danny, Luz, and the shooter were sitting, the car slowed and stopped.

"Buenas tardes," Danny said in his best holiday fashion, looking up at the late sun and guessing it was still *tardes*.

The passenger-side cop said the same thing back and grinned. "Are you here for the fiesta?" he asked in surprisingly decent English.

"Yes, it should be a good time." Danny gestured toward Luz and the shooter. "My friend already has a pretty woman to dance with. Will anybody mind if I dance with the señoritas?"

The cop laughed and looked hard at the shooter, looked at him in a pointed way, as if he were comparing a face he'd seen in a photograph to the one before him. He tried to be casual about it, but wasn't very smooth, and it was noticeable.

Then he grinned again and spoke to Danny. "Your amigo is indeed lucky to have such a pretty woman to dance with. Yes, the señoritas will dance with you if you ask politely, and they will be pleased you asked. A word of warning, though: Plan to leave the fiesta around midnight. By that time there is much beer in the bellies that muddies the minds." He flipped his head toward the hombres in back of him. "And it makes them reach for knives or beer bottles when they have an argument. If things get foolish, they surely will blame any problems on the gringos who were dancing with village women, and then you will have trouble."

"Muchas gracias," Danny said. "We'll be careful."

"Yes, be careful, amigo." The cop looked at Luz María in her yellow dress. "That is a very pretty dress, señorita. Señor, you are very lucky to have such a pretty woman in a pretty dress who cares about you." The shooter grinned back, nodding vigorously.

"We are engaged to be married," Luz said without missing a beat, and tucked her arm in the shooter's. Danny was starting to wonder about that very thing himself.

The cops rolled down the street, talking with one another. Where the plaza ended, the driver looked back at them over his shoulder, then made a corner and headed out of the village toward the Durango road.

"What do you think?" Danny asked the shooter.

"Don't know. Things are always what they are and never what they seem; there's always a lot of smoke and swirl in these situations. We'll go to the fiesta tonight, pull out in the morning. Maybe take the road to Ponuco we were on this afternoon and try to work our way north through the mountains. Is that possible?"

"It might be possible if we strap on the supplementary gas cans and if you want to take about three years to get to the border."

"If that's what it takes, that's what it takes. We'll consider that plan C. I'll pay you extra, of course."

Danny wasn't worried about money at the moment. He was worried about the forces of light roaming around the state of Sinaloa, like beaters moving through a forest. He was worried that the thin, hard face of Clayton Price might have been staring out of some photograph along the road in Concordia while cops passed it from hand to hand and committed it to memory before driving through the nearby villages on a festival day in 1993.

Then he got to thinking the shooter had said "plan C."

"If that's plan C, maybe you'd like to share plans A and B with me?"

"Plan B is a straight run up the main roads, take our chances. I'm still thinking about plan A. I'll let you know when I get it worked out." He went inside and came back with a margarita for Luz and two beers for him and Danny.

Luz poked Danny's arm. "I washed your shirt, Danny. Pants, too, so you will look nice for the fiesta. I hang them in window to dry. Such two handsome hombres — the señoritas will be chasing both of you, and I will be jealous."

There was a curious lilt in her voice Danny had never heard before, something to do with getting a fix on things and knowing who you are and where you're going. At least she was still doing the laundry.

While Luz was up in the room getting herself ready, the shooter told Danny how he'd felt about hearing the rosary being said at twilight. It was the most thoughtful Danny had ever seen him.

He suggested they visit a man named Ian who lived up the hill back of where they were staying. The shooter had reconnoitered the village on Saturday morning. Outside of a house he'd seen a sign proclaiming Ian Somebody lived within and had published a book called *"The Treasure of the Sierra Madre" Continued.* The shooter said B. Traven's original book was one of his favorites, the quintessential portrait of greed and treachery, but he'd never heard about any sequel and wanted to see what this guy Ian was up to. After a field trip in the afternoon, Danny was thinking, they were now into the archaeology of Sierra Madrean literature.

The visit to Ian's turned out to be interesting in the old macabre sense, in the way the Chinese curse you by saying "May you live in interesting times." Ian had cancer of the face, a common problem for fair-skinned gringos who don't wear wide-brimmed hats while wandering around in the Mexican sun. And Ian's case was a bad one, the front half of his nose missing along with other nasty mutilations. But he was glad to see them. In fact, he was elated they'd dropped by and brought out two more glasses so they could share the tequila he'd been working on for some time. Both Danny and the shooter said they'd pass on the tequila, but Ian poured their glasses full anyway. It's hard to drink alone all the time.

Danny couldn't help staring at Ian's face,

couldn't get by that at first. Pretty rough, especially where you could see right up his nose. He tried to distract himself by looking around Ian's digs, but it was hard not to stare at the man's face. After a minute or two of that incivility, Danny knocked back his tequila in one shot, let it take hold, and started to feel better. In ten minutes or so he was able to stop looking at the holes in Ian's face, avoid the aqueous eyes, and concentrate on what he was saying.

Ian had done a lot of things in his time. Evidently he'd made some real money in Texas land development and plowed the profits into a huge mining venture with the Mexican government as his partner. Said he'd wandered all over central Mexico in a Chevy Blazer, looking for silver. It'd all gone to hell, and Ian had lost everything, including his face and his wife, who'd died of diabetes several years back. He seemed jovial enough, but Danny could sense the laughter was a shallow and transparent mask for the sorrows of his losses — his face, his wife, his money.

Though something about it didn't ring true to Danny, Ian claimed his Christian name meant "God is gracious" and repeated over and over, "Can't complain . . . Christ, I've had a good life." He'd say that, then would take another hit of tequila and complain some more, and later on would come back to saying his life had been a good life.

Indeed he'd written a sequel to *The Treasure of the Sierra Madre* and had sent it to a New York literary shark who claimed to be an agent and who'd agreed to read the manuscript for a fee of $700. The agent had written back, saying Ian gave evidence of real literary talent, but the book wasn't publishable in its present form, probably wasn't fixable, and that Ian ought to set it aside and start on another writing project. The agent would be happy to read anything else Ian wrote, for another $700 or so. But Ian was broke; he didn't have $700, he didn't even have another manuscript or an idea for one. Danny could empathize with him.

The shooter mentioned that Danny was a writer. That got Ian's attention, and he spoke excitedly: "What have you written? Anything I might've heard of?"

Danny didn't want to get into a discussion of the writing business, since he knew the next thing Ian would want was the name and phone number of Danny's literary agent. Martha already had manuscripts, dozens and maybe hundreds, from Ians all over the world who wanted to get published. The manuscripts lay neatly stacked in a corner of her office, waiting to be taken to the incinerator, unread.

Danny looked at his watch and said it was about time to collect Luz and get on to the dance.

"Wait a minute!" Ian pleaded, wailing almost, and pouring Danny another shot of tequila. "Tell me what you've written."

"Not too much, a few things here and there. Nothing anybody's ever heard of."

Danny started feeling pinched and claustrophobic and wanted out of there, wanted music and lights, wanted to dance with Luz María and feel her body against him. He stood up as Ian started rambling on about a computer he'd bought from some off-the-wall outfit ten years before. The machine used diskettes of a size nobody made anymore. He had all sixty of his diskettes filled, and did they know where he could get any more? They didn't, and Danny started walking down the stairs from Ian's place, feeling not at all festive with the fiesta getting under way.

The shooter paused at the stair top. "Ian, if we wanted to take a real scenic route up to the border, wander through Mexico on back roads, is there any way we could do it?"

Suspicions confirmed. Danny'd had a feeling the shooter was interested in Ian for something other than literary purposes. Ian said they should come back and sit down, have some more tequila, and he'd tell them what he knew about the Mexican outback, and he knew a lot. Besides, an hombre called Gustavo was coming by in a while to play dominoes and they could ask him about scenic routes, too.

Ian slugged down a double, or maybe triple, shot of tequila and was starting to look a little crazylike, so both Danny and the shooter begged off, mentioning Luz was waiting for them. On their way down the stairs, Ian said pretty much the same thing Danny had told the shooter. It was possible to get just about anywhere in Mexico, using back roads, particularly if you had four-wheel drive. But you had to know what you were doing, and if you didn't, you'd end up out of gas and out of water and out of time, not having the slightest idea of where to get any of those.

He flailed about with his arms. "You can die out there, every bad thing you can think of: snakes, scorpions, sun." He swept his hand in a wide arc of almost three hundred sixty degrees. "Mexico's a sonuvabitch in the outback. Matter of fact, it's a sonuvabitch anywhere, doesn't cut you any slack at all. Look what it's done to me."

So much for plan C. That left them with

taking the main highways or sailing along on the shooter's still secret plan A. Danny could hear music and see colored lights hanging across a cement dance floor down the hillside from Ian's. It was time to party, maybe for the last time, at least for a while.

As Danny and the shooter opened the gate to Ian's place and headed down the path to the cantina, Ian called after them, "Hey, stop back tomorrow, talk some more. Remember the great adversary of art or anything else is a hurried life. As they used to teach us in World War Two, the eight enemies of survival are fear, pain, cold, thirst, hunger, fatigue, boredom, and loneliness. Haste is the ninth."

"You're sure, now. It was him?" Walter McGrane had taken a four-hour nap in the afternoon and was feeling better, alert and wanting to get the job done and get the goddamn hell out of Mexico and back to civilization. He spoke sharply to the policeman before him, smelling chiles when the man burped.

"Señor, it was him, I'm sure. He sat there on the cantina porch."

The other policeman was shaking his head up and down in spirited confirmation of what his partner was saying.

"And there was a man and a woman with him?"

"*Sí.*"

"And the woman was a Mexican, and pretty?"

"Oh, yes, señor. Very pretty." With his hands, he carved the shape of a svelte woman in the air and grinned.

"What did the other man look like?"

The policeman shrugged and held out his palms. "He looked like any other gringo. *Norteamericano*, I think."

Walter McGrane turned to the windbreakered men behind him. "Get saddled up. We'll go in at dawn."

The men in windbreakers nodded and smiled at each other.

Slow Waltz in Zapata

Luz was standing on the cantina porch when the shooter and Danny returned from Ian's place. She'd borrowed an iron and had pressed her yellow dress, bathed, and washed her black hair, letting it hang straight and long. A pale orange hibiscus was fastened just behind her left ear. Up close and over time, even the exotic becomes common and un-beheld, and in the daily slog of life, Danny sometimes forgot how beautiful Luz María could be. She had a beauty all her own, warm and unaffected, almost the peasant but with a hint of something more — on the borderline of regal, maybe.

As he and the shooter rounded a corner and saw her on the cantina porch, Danny realized he'd always thought of her as a girl. But along the way, María de la Luz Santos had become a woman in all the dimensions that defined a woman, and Danny had some-how missed the transformation.

The shooter couldn't stop looking at her, stood there locked down and staring, until he caught himself. He cleared his throat and sat on the porch railing, scuffling dust around with his desert boot, looking first at his feet, then up at the curve of night and the stars sprinkled across it.

Danny said, "You look as good as it gets, Luz, and better than that."

She smiled at him, hooked her left arm in his, her right arm in the shooter's, and the three of them walked slowly along the cobblestones to a place where music was playing.

The dance was held in an area called *el centro*, near the plaza. It was more or less an open-air community center, thirty feet wide and fifty long, with concrete walls on all sides and a concrete floor, and a basketball hoop at one end.

As they entered the dancing grounds, Danny looked up the hill behind *el centro*. A hundred feet above and off to the right, he could see Ian and someone else — the friend, Gustavo, apparently — drinking and playing dominoes beneath the yellow orange of an overhead light. Ian tipped back his head and took a long drink of tequila, hearing the music float up from the dancing place, remembering the dreams of silver he'd followed through the canyons of Mexico. Christ, it hadn't been a bad life, not all that bad, and

God was gracious when tequila allowed Him to be.

The band had arrived in a green Volkswagen Beetle. How they'd stuffed two guitars, a trumpet, an accordion, and a stand-up bass in there, along with five people, wasn't clear. But they'd done it, and they were here, the music filling *el centro* and the night.

Hombres in straw cowboy hats and clean shirts paraded around, beers in hand. The señoritas sat in small groups on the far side of the concrete floor, a few of them almost as pretty as Luz and ready to drive men to their knees in prayer just from the looking at them and the contemplating all that is possible with a woman on a night like this. Little boys in white shirts and black pants ran and slid on the dance floor. So did little girls in white dresses and white shoes. The dancing was slow to get started, reminding Danny of the old high school affairs back in Kansas, where the girls sat along one wall waiting for the heroes to whip up enough nerve to ask them to dance.

By about nine-thirty a few couples were moving around the floor and others were looking as if they might. Danny asked Luz if she'd like to give it a try. They slid into the music, dancing nice and easy to a slow waltz, trumpet and accordion playing fine old

250

Mexican harmonies. Luz smelled like all the flowers that had ever followed rain and felt good in his arms, and instantly he wanted to haul her off to bed. He wanted her at that moment more than he'd ever wanted her, wanted her panting and naked, to bend her like grass in a summer wind and pull her back toward him from wherever she seemed to be going. He brought her in close and told her what he was thinking. As the song declined, she smiled with her mouth and her eyes in a way hinting everything was possible and forthcoming.

They danced a fast number, one of those Mexican polkas whose rhythms eluded Danny, but Luz laughed and took the lead, pulling him around the floor and getting it done. Danny was sweating, yet Luz still seemed as cool as she'd looked on the cantina porch. They walked over to where the shooter was leaning against the wall. As they approached him, he smiled and applauded quietly.

"Very nice," he said.

Danny veered off toward a little stand on the far side of the dance floor. Walking past the señoritas sitting in a row, he grinned at them, and they giggled when he said, *"Buenas noches, señoritas."* The hombres near the beer stand didn't giggle when he greeted them, but they didn't seem all that unfriendly, either, saying, *"Buenas noches,"* back to him and tugging on their Pacíficos. While Danny waited at the concession stand, he could hear one of them saying something about "two gringos, one woman." The others laughed, their imaginations working images of what two gringos and one woman might bring about later on in the village darkness.

The band took a break. Luz, Danny, and the shooter stood near the south wall of *el centro,* not saying much, enjoying the laughter and swirl of people. The village priest came in and greeted everyone. That quieted things down, beers sheepishly hid behind pant legs. When *el padrecito* left after making his rounds, things picked up again. Danny watched him go and watched the bottles of Pacífico re-appear, and he thought about how lovable hypocrisy could be sometimes; it had such a human quality.

There came a moment when Danny gen-uinely felt sorry for the shooter, the only time he would ever truly feel that way about him. Danny and Luz had danced again, then walked back to where Clayton Price was still leaning against the concrete wall. She held out her arms to him, indicating she was will-ing to dance with him. He shook his head and smiled timidly.

She coaxed, and he finally said, almost in a whisper, "I've never danced."

Danny stared at him. "C'mon, not ever? Somewhere, sometime, you must have danced?"

"No. Not ever. That's the truth."

Strange, how very goddamned strange. In a world full of people dancing, here was a man in his fifties who'd never held a woman in his arms while music played. He was, indeed, a creature even more rare than Danny had imagined. Danny wasn't all that good on a dance floor, but he'd spent a lot of nights doing it. A little beer, a little music, holding a woman close, good things to come along afterward.

Clayton Price looked down at his dusty shoes. "It's just I've never been anyplace where it all worked out . . . you know, music and somebody to dance with. I haven't spent my life in those kinds of places." He looked up, implacability shed for a moment, as if he were asking — one time and this one time only — for a moment of understanding about where and how he'd gone, of all the things he'd never been. Of all the things he'd never had, white porch swings on Kansas summer nights and the voice of a girl on her way to becoming a woman, telling you about her dreams and the new sweater she'd bought

253

for the cold nights ahead.

And Danny thought back to the fraternity brawls in Columbia, Missouri, where he'd twisted the night away with Missy Morganthal to the repetitious beat of Chubby Checker and Bo Diddley. Somewhere around that time, Clayton Price would have been lying thousands of miles to the west, in warm jungle rain, ants crawling up his legs and mosquitoes drawing blood from his face, his hands touching the wood and steel of a deathstick. Clayton Price going into his bubble while Danny was playing grab-ass with a mostly drunk coed named Missy. One night Missy had stripped down to nothing and had done a wild version of the twist while her sorority sisters had rolled their eyes and Danny's fraternity brothers had gone into a tribal thump, urging her on to greater heights and screaming like men with stone hatchets and wars to fight.

At that moment, half a world away, the shooter might have been watching a woman not much older than Missy through his Redfield scope, watching her squat down to pee just before he blew her head apart at seven hundred yards when the fog lifted. Christ, no wonder Clayton Price had never learned to dance. And Danny Pastor felt sorry for the thin man, while simultaneously feeling guilty again for reasons not altogether clear to him.

"I will teach you to dance, don't be afraid." Luz was looking up at the shooter, soft little smile on her face. She was speaking so quietly Danny could barely hear her. "We will wait for a slow song."

If it were left to women such as Luz, we'd be a better species. Danny started reflecting on that certainty. Here was a man, Clayton Price, who seemed oblivious of committing the most violent acts possible, who probably had never loved with any duration or intensity, and who was brought low now merely by the thought of moving around to music with a woman in his arms. And Luz María standing there, willing to tackle the problem in a soft, loving way. Ready to teach the boy a little more about being a man, something that had to be done gradually, in the way women know how to do it. If men let them.

A fast song, then another one of those slow waltzes the Mexicans played so well, accordion taking the lead. The night was warm and humid. Clayton Price had sweat beading up on his forehead and throat, from the heat . . . maybe . . . more likely from the fear of dancing.

Without being obvious about it, Luz took

him along the concrete to an area of the floor where it was quiet and the hombres couldn't see them very well. Underneath magenta bougainvillea hanging over the wall, she put her left hand on his shoulder, placed his right hand behind her waist, and took his left hand in her right. They moved slowly, out of time to the music at first, then gradually onto the beat.

The shooter was clumsy but stayed with it, embarrassed and yet giving it a try. His long legs were stiff and unsure, his desert boots shuffled around in unusual ways, but Luz persisted and somehow it sort of worked. It worked because of Luz and because the shooter cared for her in ways he didn't really understand, because he had come somewhere along the way to want music and softness and didn't know how or where to look for it until he'd met Luz. Whatever happened out ahead, Danny thought, Clayton Price could say he'd danced one warm night in the Sierra Madre with a woman who wore a pale orange hibiscus in her black hair. Danny couldn't help smiling, and it was odd, real odd, but he had tears in his eyes as he watched them.

The song ended, and they walked back toward Danny. Luz was smiling; so was the shooter smiling in a shy fashion. He lit a cigarette and leaned against the wall where he'd been leaning before and couldn't get that little smile off his face, just kept it there as if it were involuntary. He was holding on to the moment, pressing it like a flower into his memory.

Luz and the shooter danced a few more times, always to slow songs. Danny looked over the lineup of señoritas who didn't seem to be attached to anyone and asked one of them to dance. She was wearing a red print dress and heavy-looking black high heels, her hair gathered in the back with a metal clasp. Her friends giggled, and she looked at them, slightly flustered but pleased the aging gringo had asked her, taking Danny's hand when he held it out. She had a thin line of perspiration along her upper lip and smelled warm and honest, like the earth itself after the sun had beat upon it for a long summer day.

She was called Nacha and spoke no English. But she and Danny got around the floor just fine. He took her back after two songs, thanked her, and asked another señorita who was sitting next to her. Eventually he worked his way down the line — the thin ones and heavy ones, pretty and otherwise — and, given he didn't know when or if ever he might dance again, there was something es-

pecially good and true about dancing with
a row of señoritas on a warm May evening
in the middle of his life.

THE RUN FOR EL NORTE

Danny, Luz, and the shooter left the dance shortly after midnight when things were starting to heat up a bit. Two of the hombres had begun pushing each other around over in one corner of the floor a few minutes earlier, and it was time to go. They walked along the cobblestones toward their rooms, stopped for a moment, and looked at a quarter moon rocking in the southwest, out across the foothills of the Sierra Madre. Luz was humming a tune the band had played, and Danny was sure it was the song to which she and Clayton Price had first danced.

But the dancing wasn't finished. They passed an open doorway, and inside a woman held a baby high in the light of a bare, single bulb, singing to the baby as she moved slowly around a small room in waltz time. Around the room she danced and the baby in its white nightshirt smiling down at the woman's face and gurgling with pleasure. Danny looked at the shooter who was looking at Luz who was smiling. All of them felt as if they were spying on something so private it belonged only to the woman and the baby, and they walked on. They'd seen some old, old dance neither Danny Pastor nor Clayton Price understood very well. But women understand that kind of thing; Luz understood, and Danny hurt for her, guessing she was remembering a hot July day in Puerto Vallarta when she'd done something she hadn't wanted to do because he'd insisted, and he'd bought her a Panasonic tape player afterward. And he was sorry for that, too. Over the last few days, Danny Pastor had started to feel sorry about a lot of things.

Danny was tired, but the shooter and Luz seemed reluctant to let the evening close. Eventually, though, they went to their separate rooms, where Danny and Luz made love. It was good, as always, but there was something a little distant about her, as if she were someplace else even while she pressed her belly against his.

He awakened when full dawn was somewhere east of the mountains, silence and a night world outside. Luz was gone. She came in a few minutes later, naked and walking soft, lying down beside Danny, who said nothing and feigned sleep. She lay there softly humming the same tune she'd been humming a few hours earlier. And something in the sound of her told Danny she was smiling.

Danny slept again, an hour maybe, coming awake when he heard loud and urgent knocking on their door.

"Yes, yes, hold on," yanking up his jeans.

Clayton Price, standing there with first light coming up behind him. The roosters and donkeys were in full chorus, and dogs were fighting somewhere down the street, sounding like wolves as they tore at one another.

"Get up and get ready to move," the shooter said. "Right now."

"What's wrong?"

"Don't know. Something's not right, got bad feelings in my gut. I'm going to look around. I'll be back in five minutes. Be ready when I get here."

Danny shook Luz into consciousness. When the shooter returned, they were dressed, scratchy with sleep but waking up fast. Luz sat on the bed, Danny leaned on the washstand, feeling the bulge of the twenty-five hundred dollars he'd taken out of its sleeping-bag hiding place and stuffed in the left front pocket of his jeans. The shooter closed the door and stood there in his jeans, denim shirt, and photographer's vest. On the wall behind and above his head a small gecko lizard glued itself to the adobe, tail toward the ceiling and silent and still, waiting for something of worth to pass its way.

"I made a phone call last night. Went down and got the shopkeeper out of bed, said it was an emergency. I called a guy in Monterrey." He nodded toward Danny. "Called him the other day while you were in Mazatlán and made some preliminary arrangements. He's an old friend of mine from the military, high placed now in the U.S. diplomatic service. I saved his ass in the jungle one time and he owes me. I asked him about this whole situation. He told me because I hit the naval officer in Puerto Vallarta, word is out that I'm a loose cannon, no longer to be trusted, and that I might be in the process of settling old scores all over the place. That's why you saw the official-looking gringos in Concordia. They're real bad guys, CIA or worse. My Monterrey contact says everybody's after us — after me, at least. I didn't say anything about the two of you. On the other hand, there's plenty of people who've seen the three of us together over the last few days. In any case, this is starting to look like Cortés's march out of Tenochtitlán."

The shooter again amazed Danny; now he was citing Mexican history. Worse, he was beginning to see himself as Hernán Cortés when the Mexica tried to stop him by breaching a causeway linking his island redoubt to the mainland. That mapping made Luz into Cortés's concubine, Malinche. And Danny . . . Danny into what? Driver, foot soldier at the worst. Chicago had never been like this. There, Danny had gone back to his apartment at night after interviewing the local wiseguys. This was different — he couldn't go home and put on his pajamas and Dave Brubeck.

The shooter was still talking, little grin on his face, almost as if he were enjoying this. Christ, maybe he is, Danny thought. He started wondering if Clayton Price had put himself into this situation just so he could work his way out or maybe he didn't want to get out at all. Danny took refuge in the thought that Cortés had made it across the causeway with at least some of his force intact and listened to the shooter talk.

"Here's how it lies. I don't think there's a chance in hell we can get out of this by road. According to my source in Monterrey, the main highways are roadblocked and anybody who even looks suspicious is being hauled in. I had to call in all my chits, but I've managed to arrange for a chopper to pick me up. That's why I made the call last night, to get confirmation. It's coming in about twenty minutes. It'll fly me up over the border, refueling on the way, and set me down outside of Brownsville. From there I'll make a run for wherever I can get to."

He was talking crisp, giving a military briefing, getting his endgame under way. "The chopper will come in from the east over the mountains and land in a clearing at a mine entrance below the village. Luz and I were down there the other day."

Danny remembered what Luz had said on Saturday, that the shooter had made a telephone call and kept saying, "LC, silver mine." She was close. What he was saying was, "LZ, silver mine" — landing zone at the silver mine.

"You have a choice." He was looking at Danny. "Come along on the chopper or try and drive the Bronco out of here. By the time they figure out what's going on, you should be back in Puerto Vallarta, telling people you took a little trip around the countryside to see some places you'd never seen, had a scrap with your girlfriend, and she went off somewhere on her own. Oh, yes, one other thing. Taped to the back of your toilet in Puerto Vallarta is the gun I used to make the hit there. You might want to get rid of it."

"You mean you were going to frame me with the killing?"

"It wasn't a bad idea. You saw me make

the hit, I tip off the cops about the gun after I get to the States. They find the gun and arrest you, throw you in the slammer while they sort it out. I doubt if they would have actually believed you did it, but if they couldn't find anyone else, the gun would be more than enough evidence to put you away or hang you or whatever they do down here. That way they could say they'd found their man and close the book on it."

"You *bastard.*"

The shooter smiled. "Like I said before, it's a tough, cruel game. But you've done your part, and I'm giving you absolution and freedom. By the way, Luz wants to come north with me."

"Like *hell!*"

"Ask her."

Danny looked at Luz, and she nodded, clear eyed and ready to go with him. "Why, for chrissake?" He already knew — Luz wanted *el Norte,* and the shooter was her postage — but asked the question anyway.

She didn't say anything, glanced over at the shooter.

He said, "I'm not sure *I'm* capable of loving at all. But, Danny, *you* love too timidly. I don't know which is worse. You have this offhand way of treating her most of the time, as if she's a partially reformed street whore.

. . . She told me about her past. She says I treat her with respect. You figure it out."

Danny took a long, shaky breath and looked out the window for a moment, then over at Luz and noticed she was wearing the shooter's bracelet.

He saw where Danny was looking. "The bracelet has a four-ounce gold nugget under the blue coloring. If things go bad, she's got traveling money."

The shooter hesitated for a moment, letting the new arrangements sink in and settle down, then dug in his pocket and handed a roll of bills to Danny. "Here's the rest of the five thousand I owe you. Make up your mind, Danny Pastor. I scouted around for a few minutes and didn't see anything out there, but I've learned to trust my gut, and my gut doesn't feel good this morning. Come with us if you want. We'll blow up the Bronco with gasoline on our way out. If that doesn't work for you, take the Bronco and make a run for it. By yourself you'll probably make it; nobody's looking for a lone gringo."

"What's your gut telling you?" Danny asked.

"Not sure. I thought I heard something up on the highway, what sounded like gears grinding on one of those old deuce-and-a-half troop carriers. I walked around a bit,

266

didn't see anything. But, doing what I do, there's a sixth sense you develop over the years. And you pay attention to those feelings."

"What do you *think* is happening?"

The shooter looked at his watch. "The chopper'll be here in fifteen minutes. Like I said, not sure. If I had to guess, I'd say those cops last night recognized me. You saw the way they looked . . ."

Clayton Price never finished his sentence, pausing and cocking his head toward the sound of boots in the interior courtyard below the room. He tugged up his pant leg and pulled the Beretta, cracked the door, and looked out.

Then, turning for a moment toward Luz and Danny, with that half-and-hard smile of his, some old bowstring inside him coming back taut enough to snap, and said, "It's gonna be a sonuvabitch." He went down on his belly and opened the door, crawling toward the edge of the balcony.

Danny could hear voices below and see the shooter holding the Beretta in both hands, steadying it. The sound of it going off in the enclosed courtyard was like a howitzer. He shot three more times and jumped to his feet. "Now! Follow me!"

Danny's decision point, another branch in

the complicated tree that had begun in El Niño six nights ago. He could have just hunkered down behind one of the beds and tried to explain his way out of it later on. But he never considered that for some reason and obeyed the shooter's orders without hesitating. It seemed like the right thing to do then, the force and energy of time-present subverting other alternatives.

They ran along the balcony and down the stairs. Three men dressed in uniforms of the Mexican army were lying on the tile, rifles scattered around. Two had holes in their faces, the third was bleeding from the chest and was tossing about, moaning.

They made it to the cantina doorway and looked out. More uniforms were moving through the plaza trees, across the narrow street directly in front of them.

The shooter was talking fast. "There's a side door out through the kitchen. Take the hillside path to the silver mine. Luz knows where it is. Wait for me there. Stay low; there'll be some serious people outside who'll take down anything they feel like."

He grabbed Danny's shoulder, looked at him straight on, and grinned again in that strange, hard way of his, face crinkled but eyes serious. "We should've bought the goddamned ocelot . . . should've done that,

Danny Pastor. See you at the silver mine."

He gave Danny a get-going push and turned to the front door of the cantina. Danny grabbed Luz and followed orders. They went out through the kitchen and hunkered down behind some bushes. Four soldiers came off the plaza and walked toward the cantina, three of them with rifles leveled at the front door and the fourth carrying an automatic weapon. Having watched the shooter work before and knowing he prioritized the enemy's firepower, Danny said to himself, "The bozo with the automatic weapon will get it first." He did and went down, clutching his throat with bloody hands as the shooter's gun snapped.

Then a high, hard fist slapped Zapata, setting free again all the ancient furies a mountain village had seen in its long past — the French, the Spanish, the Mexican army. And once again Zapata exploded into a dust storm of noise and chaos and cruelty.

Of the four soldiers who had approached the cantina, the remaining three ran back toward the trees in the plaza. The Beretta again, and one of them fell, spinning around as he hit the cobblestones. At the same time more soldiers and what looked like *federales* were running up the street from the west, coming by *el centro* where Luz and Danny and Clayton Price had danced last night.

As Danny Pastor will tell you, if he hadn't been so damned scared at the time, he could have seen it all as a thing of beauty. The images are still crystalline, and he eventually has come to see it that way, as a thing of terrible beauty, when he thinks back on what occurred.

The shooter came off the cantina porch, running low to the ground and firing. He made it to the corner of the plaza and took out one of the *federales* galloping along in cowboy boots. From there, it became a violent ballet. Shooter running . . . and jumping . . . running and jumping gracefully over the fence surrounding the plaza . . . through the trees. Sound of weapons firing every which way. Bullets digging into adobe walls around the plaza or slicing leaves and bark from trees, windows shattering.

From his hiding place, Danny could somehow admire the shooter at that moment, saw him as an old lion surrounded by jackals or maybe a bull at one of Coria's bloody festivals, take your choice. He was hedged in, but under control and fighting, no panic that Danny could see. It was a place he'd been before. Danny lost count, but Clayton Price was knocking down soldiers as they ran toward him, killing some, wounding others.

Places his shots . . . one at a time . . .
   not every shot is a
      killing shot . . . but every one of
      them seems to hit a man.
            . . . Clayton Price moving . . .
shots from left . . . spin . . .
   return fire . . .
      That low-crouching run of his . . .
      through the trees,
sputter of automatic weapons . . .
   no quarter given . . .
   final stuff . . . hard stuff
      . . . hard and cruel and no quarter
      taken . . . sunlight . . . bright
         morning . . . two burros, wild
         in streets . . .
one of them running through a machine-
gun burst . . . falling . . . kicking
      on the cobblestones and screaming
      a dying burro scream, horrible
         sound . . .
shooter in behind gazebo
      . . . windbreakered man in the
      church doorway, bracing an
         unusual-looking rifle against the
         stone next to him and thinking
one shot, one kill . . .

The soldiers retreated and began taking the
gazebo apart stone by stone with automatic

weapons fire. A white van roared into the plaza area. The burro lying in the street caused the driver to swerve, and Walter McGrane covered his face as the van smashed through the plaza fence and into a tree. Another man in a windbreaker crawled out the rear door of the van, staggered to his feet, and began a hobbled run, swinging a short-barreled Remington shotgun in an arc before him. A Mexican soldier, wild and panicked and shooting at anything approximating a hostile target, opened up on the man in the windbreaker, who took him down with one blast from the Remington. An internecine firefight erupted, with other soldiers turning their guns on the windbreaker, thinking he was the man they'd come for. The Remington blew apart another soldier, before the windbreaker shouted loud enough in expletive Spanish that he was not the target.

The shooter was crawling fast, away from the gazebo and south toward the fence surrounding the plaza. Danny could see a man in the church doorway, looking down the scope of a rifle pointed toward the plaza fence only thirty yards away. At that moment the rifle jerked upward without firing, the village priest struggling with the rifleman, screaming about the desecration of the place where Jesus lived.

Clayton Price saw the priest and the rifleman and knew he'd come within a second or two of dying there in the grass. He made the fence, staying low and looking over his shoulder, hearing the automatic weapons still firing at the gazebo, splinters of stone flying into the air from hundreds of bullets. The sniper finally disengaged himself from the priest and hit him full across the nose with a quick hand chop. As the priest fell, the man brought the rifle up again and was scoping for his target when the slug from Clayton Price's Beretta slammed into his chest. He staggered back into the church darkness as Clayton Price came to his feet and ran for the door where the sniper had been standing.

Danny saw the shooter running toward the church, saw him make the door and dart inside, probably heading out the side entrance and down the hill behind the church.

Luz and Danny began running along the hillside path, hidden from the plaza area by trees and houses. They hurdled a sow and her piglets lying in the middle of the path. The sow got up, grunting, piglets squealing.

The path forked. Luz pointed right, and they ran that way, starting to go downhill. She stumbled and fell on loose gravel, rolling fifteen feet down the slope, tearing herself on rocks and ripping her blouse. As Danny pulled her up, he heard the *thuk-thuk* of a helicopter coming in low through a cut in the mountains. They were above the main part of the village, and Danny stood there for a few seconds, trying to get a fix on what was happening. Below him and Luz, and closer to the landing zone than they were, he could see the shooter down on one knee, reloading clips. Christ, one little short-barreled pistol. He was holding off a small invasion force with it, but Danny could see it was going to be over soon unless they made the chopper. There were too many on the other side, too many bad guys, even for Clayton Price.

A gringo in a blue windbreaker was creeping toward the shooter, shotgun held ready. Soldiers were following the shotgun man, being cautious now. Danny was sure the shotgun was going to get Clayton Price, who was still pushing ammunition into clips. And it was curious . . . curious how Danny's allegiances were somehow shifting, away from the forces of light and toward something else. He had the feeling he should call out to Clayton Price, warn him about what was coming behind him, be part of the old American custom favoring the underdog in all things.

But Clayton Price didn't need Danny's help. He scrambled behind a bush, jammed a clip into the Beretta, went to his belly, and waited until he saw shotgun man's feet. The Beretta popped and a bullet blew into the man's right knee. As the man staggered and instinctively reached downward to touch shattered bone, the shooter came out low and hit the man with another round. The man staggered and fell forward, the business end of his Remington pumpgun plunging into the earth and simultaneously discharging, blowing up in his face. The soldiers behind retreated and went to ground, wondering what the hell they were doing in the middle of a bunch of crazy gringos trying to kill each other.

The shooter was running again, heading toward the silver mine. Luz and Danny began to move fast, Luz bleeding on her face and arms and back from the fall. Helicopter coming in, getting ready to set down. They met up with the shooter fifty yards from the landing zone. He had wide sweat circles under his arms, the denim shirt sticking to him and bloody on one shoulder. He'd been hit, but not bad, evidently. He looked like a big cat, moved like one, some kind of curious light in his eyes, wild and yet focused, his chest pumping for air, out on the rice paddies again.

The three of them crouched there, looking around. Behind them, soldiers had seen the helicopter landing and, regrouped by an officer, were creeping through scrub trees and brush toward the silver mine.

"This is it! Move!" the shooter hissed. He grabbed Luz's hand and started running toward the chopper settling onto the gravel at the mine entrance, rotor blades blowing brown dust up and around it.

Coming to his feet, Danny slipped on loose stones, got up, slipped again, and followed Luz and the shooter, who were already fifteen yards ahead of him. Gunshots from behind, small poofs of earth where the bullets hit. Through blowing dust and the sweat running into his eyes, Danny could see Luz and the shooter up ahead, Luz in almost total fatigue, being dragged by an arrow named Clayton Price.

We might make it, Danny thought. We might make it . . . we're going to make it, *by God.*

"Run, Luz!" Danny screamed.

The cargo door on the chopper slid open. Through the swirl of dust Danny could see two men squatting inside, and both men were pointing automatic weapons directly at Luz and Clayton Price. And the men were firing the weapons, not over Luz's and the shooter's heads, but *at* them and at Danny. Danny hit the ground at full tilt, sliding along on sharp gravel, tearing his chest. Ahead of him the shooter skidded to a stop and started pulling Luz back in Danny's direction. She was confused, Clayton Price shouting at her to run back the way they'd come.

Oh no — Danny was screaming inside himself — oh *no!* . . . goddammit *no!* — not this, not Luz.

The line of fire from the chopper swept across Luz and the shooter like a big, invisible knife blade. They jerked and spun, stumbled and went down, the shooter still holding on to her hand, blood coming from her face. The shooter wrapped himself around Luz, covering her, aiming his pistol toward the chopper. He scrubbed one of the men with his second shot. The other man ducked back inside the cargo bay out of sight.

The shooter struggled to his feet, somehow he did that, pulling Luz with him. A bullet had sliced across and through her cheek, and she was bleeding from three other places on her chest, but she was still alive, and Danny could see her clawing Clayton Price's shirt, grabbing his hair, her head lolling from side to side, only vaguely aware of what was happening, death-terror and instinct taking over.

He lifted her onto his left shoulder, her legs to the front of him, and began stumbling toward Danny. And lastingly curls that memory in the mind of Danny Pastor, the image of Clayton Price carrying Luz María through the morning dust, his legs splayed and beginning to buckle but still coming on and refusing to cease what it was Clayton Price did best. And never, ever, in the times to come, would Danny forget the look on the shooter's face at that moment — bleeding from a half dozen parts of his body and with one ear nearly missing, he was no longer human but something else altogether, gone completely feral, eyes crazy-wide with a transcending agony all their own and looking not at Danny but somewhere back of Danny, living now in another place only a man such as Clayton Price could ever understand. With Luz balanced on one shoulder, he brought the Beretta up and began firing over Danny's head at whatever was coming from behind.

Danny rolled into a brushy ditch and yelled, "This way!" The shooter, vest and pants and shirt blood soaked, eyes glazed over and someplace else, nonetheless heard him and started toward where Danny was lying. There wasn't much left of the woman over his shoulder, the soft, brown woman who only a few hours before had been wearing a flower in her hair and a yellow dress and dancing with a man who had never danced before. Luz María was no longer moving, eyes opalescent and head dangling in a lifeless way even as Clayton Price carried her.

An automatic weapon in the chopper's cargo bay opened up again. The shooter stumbled and went to his knees, somehow got back to his feet once more, still balancing Luz on his shoulder. Danny could see bullets marching through the dust and then up and through Clayton Price and Luz. As the bullets cut into them, Clayton Price twisted toward the chopper and tried to aim the Beretta, but what had once been his face disappeared instantly in a spray of flesh and bone. He fell a few feet from the ditch, Luz tumbling from his shoulder. The two of them lay tangled, their bodies jerking as a burst from the automatic weapon made one final pass over them. After that, the soldiers began firing at the helicopter, and the automatic weapon inside the cargo door turned its attention to them.

The helicopter lifted off, and it never has been clear to Danny just who was on what side that morning. In all the confusion nobody apparently knew who was an ally and who was the enemy, so everybody had simply started shooting at everyone else. The soldiers on the ground hadn't been told the chopper was on their side, or maybe somebody didn't want them to know. Or maybe it wasn't, maybe there were three sides. After a while, it didn't make any difference.

Danny checked himself. Chest bleeding bad from where he'd slid on the rocks, but all right otherwise. He called out for the shooter, for Luz. No answer. He didn't expect one. From where the two of them lay in the dust, there was only silence, and Danny was sure it would be that way forever. Clayton Price had stopped circling the ponds of autumn, had come to rest, and had taken Luz María with him.

Danny pushed up and ran along a shallow arroyo, staying low and eventually working his way up toward the main part of the village. The shooting had stopped, villagers were peering out of windows and doors at bodies littered around the plaza. Not as many bodies as it seemed to Danny when all the shooting had been taking place. Three men were down near the plaza, two who were injured slumped against the gazebo. The white Ford van was burning, black smoke rising high and fast into the mountain air. Inside the van, a gringo in a sweat-stained safari jacket lay crumpled between the rammed-back engine and his seat. Danny watched from behind a building as the van exploded and set four of the plaza's trees on fire.

Danny made it to the Bronco, put it in

four-wheel drive, and maneuvered through the jungle, then slowly climbed up a hillside northeast of the village. On the main highway, the Durango road, he looked back down into the village and beyond. Near the silver mine, men were dragging bodies through the dust, leaving dark, wet trails.

He worked on getting his head clear and drove up the highway, taking the mountain road toward Ponuco. When he got to the turnoff for the old Guadalupe church, he bumped Vito along the riverbed for a mile, where he parked it behind some brush. Don José Fierro heard the Bronco grinding over river rocks and came down to investigate. The affairs of the world were not his, and he cared nothing for what might have happened beyond the small universe over which he watched.

Danny stayed with the Keeper of Guadalupe for three days. Don José Fierro sloshed up a concoction of river mud and something else, smearing it on the deep cuts Danny had sustained from diving onto gravel. Whatever it was, it worked, and the cuts stopped bleeding. Don José gave him one of his shirts to wear, three sizes too small, but Danny was grateful and left a hundred bucks when he pulled out on the evening of the third day. The old man didn't care about money but took it and waved in the general direction of the church, indicating the money would be used for repair and maintenance.

Two miles from the Durango road, Danny stopped and got out. The cliff on which he stood dropped away for a thousand feet, ending in heavy trees and brush at the bottom. He pointed Vito toward the cliff, put the gears in neutral, and shut off the engine. Two hard pushes and the Bronco went over the side, bounced in a tear of metal on an outcropping three hundred feet down, then fell clean all the way to where it finally crashed into trees and brush. The last few days still seemed like a movie, all of it.

An hour later, Danny flagged down a bus headed for Mazatlán. The bus wound through the mountains and when it passed the village of Zapata, Danny stared straight ahead.

On the edge of Concordia, furniture makers worked in the twilight and smoke from cooking fires drifted over the highway. Children played by the roadside and brown dogs hung around restaurant tables. To Danny, thinking about the small war that had occurred in Zapata only three days past, it seemed curious somehow that life had not altered for these people. What appeared large to Danny was nothing to them. Mexico had absorbed the blows and gone on, as it always had.

A few miles east of Concordia, the bus passed through the waters of a small creek, and Danny Pastor looked upstream toward the place where he and Clayton Price and Luz had bathed a week ago. At the Pemex station south of Mazatlán, the burned remains of a white Ford van sat off to one side by itself. It was twilight, and rush hour, and there were long lines of vehicles waiting for gasoline.

YOU DO WHAT YOU CAN

Danny stopped in Mazatlán and stayed for two days in a tourist hotel, figuring nobody would pay much attention to a gringo tourist; the town was full of them. He left the room only once, to buy a couple of shirts and a new pair of jeans, some newspapers. Nothing in the papers about the shootout, but it would have been old news by then; five days had gone by since it happened. Later on there was a brief article in a regional edition of *Time* with the headline SHOOTOUT IN THE MOUNTAINS.

The piece was sketchy, stating only that a gun battle between elements of the Mexican army and a deranged ex-marine had taken place in the Mexican village of Zapata. An army commander was quoted as saying the mission was successfully completed after a brief, early morning skirmish in which no soldiers were injured and the ex-marine had been killed. In the article, the shooter was correctly identified as Clayton Price, and it was indicated not much was known about him except for his military career, which lasted eight years. There was mention of his Purple Heart and several other medals awarded for his service in Vietnam and quoted an unidentified diplomatic source as saying Mr. Price had turned into a degenerate killer after he left the military. Luz was listed only as an "unidentified Mexican woman who was the assassin's gun moll." It also said an unidentified white male was with them, but no trace of him had been found.

In Mazatlán, Danny purchased a battered Dodge pickup, using a fair chunk of the five thousand Clayton Price had given him. He headed down Route 15 toward Puerto Vallarta, stopped in Escuinapa, and bought a large flashlight along with bolt cutters and wire clippers. Through the late afternoon, he took the road west toward Teacapán and slowed down six miles out. The cage was still there under a banana tree, the ocelot still pacing. Danny parked at an abandoned pier on the lake or estuary or whatever the backwater was called and pretended to be interested in the scenery.

After dark he pulled the truck up near the ocelot and gingerly approached the cage, keeping his flashlight pointed at the ground until he reached the cage. The cat stopped pacing and snarled, lunged at the wire, and hooked a fang over it. It wasn't going to be easy.

Danny let the cat quiet down a little and decided to use the long-handled bolt cutters, closing down on the padlock holding the cage shut. The steel was low grade, and he got through it on the second try. He hooked the bolt cutters onto the door wire and swung it open, dropping the cutters and running for the truck all at the same time. The cat was out of the cage and bounding across the road toward a nearby field before Danny could shut the truck door. He watched *el gato* moving fast through moonlight, into long grass, gone.

By the following afternoon, the battered Dodge was just north of Puerto Vallarta. Danny hardly recalled the road down from Mazatlán, thinking and remembering and shaking his head at his own arrogance and how desire replaces judgment on warm nights in a Mexican beach town or, for that matter, on white porch swings in Kansas.

He made a right turn, and twenty-four miles west the road ended at the beach village of Punta de Mita. Danny bought a beer and walked out on the sand, sitting by the water's edge. In the quiet, he listened to the waves and thought about Luz, remembering how they had come here and swum naked at night.

She'd bobbed up from under the water, pushing her long black hair back over her shoulders, laughing as she'd wrapped her legs around the wild expatriate called Danny Pastor. That was a long time ago, it seemed.

Danny sat there for hours, walking back to the beach restaurant for more beer, then returning to his place in the sand. The restaurant closed and still he sat there, looking out at the rocky islands and remembering María de la Luz Santos. God, she was beautiful . . . and warm . . . and deep-down loving and all of those things for which he hadn't appreciated her enough when she was there with him. He wished then he had married her and taken her north with him. He didn't feel much like a wild expatriate anymore. He felt stupid and alone and sorry.

Danny made Puerto Vallarta and opened the door to his apartment at midnight. It was quiet and smelled a little stale, but underneath the staleness was the scent of Luz, her perfume, her body oil on the sheets. He turned on the lights and went immediately to the bathroom, looking for the gun. It wasn't there, but what *was* there was a knock on the door. He opened it: three cops and another man wearing a business suit. The suit held up a plastic bag and dangled it in Danny's face.

In the bag was the shooter's gun, the one he'd used in El Niño. Somebody had known something and had talked about it. Probably the guy who was mad at Danny for spewing oily smoke into his apartment the week before. Shit, who knows. Who cares. He heard a rumor later on, however, that the police had worked over Felipe pretty hard, and he might have said Luz and Danny had been in El Rondo the night of the killing and that they'd left with Clayton Price.

Danny got a ten-year sentence on vague charges, something about "assisting criminal elements." The assassination weapon in his apartment was fairly heavy circumstantial evidence, but they never actually charged him with the shooting itself. After a little over seventeen months in a Mexico City prison, his cell door swung open one day, and he was told he was free to go and to get the hell out of Mexico and never come back. *Vamos, ándele!* No explanation, nothing. They'd tired of feeding him, that's all he could figure out, and escorted him to the bus station, where he was given a one-way ticket for Laredo.

With Clayton Price gone, Danny had welshed on his bargain and had written up the whole adventure while he was in prison, bribing a guard to mail it on to his New

York agent. He never saw the manuscript again, never heard a thing. Maybe it didn't get to her. Maybe it did. To hell with it. It was a pretty breathless piece of writing, anyway.

Danny had kept a stash of emergency money in a Chicago bank and sent for it. With interest it came to a little over six thousand dollars. He bought another old pickup and drove it south across the border, pulling into Zapata three days later.

Nobody remembered him. He ate at the cantina and took the same room where he and Luz had stayed a year and a half earlier. Sitting on the bed, he thought about the last time they'd made love on that same bed. He walked down to the silver mine and looked around. No trace of the shootout; he didn't expect there'd be any. But scuffing in the dust, he found a rusty shell casing, small caliber. From the shooter's pistol, maybe. He stuck it in his pocket and carries it with him, some kind of talisman and some kind of warning instead of a tattoo on the thumb.

A couple of new gringos had moved into the village, and Danny talked with them later that night. They drank tequila and regaled him with stories of the great Zapata shootout, which, of course, had become part of the village's long saga and a tourist attraction in its own right. In the story, the shooter was made out to be bigger than life, which in a way he was, Danny supposed. And Luz was said to be one of the most desirable women ever to walk the earth, which in a way she was, at least that's where Danny's thinking had taken him by that time. There was only brief mention of a third person, another gringo. Nobody knew what happened to him for sure, some hearsay about him dying in prison.

One of the storytellers said, "If Gustavo comes by, he'll sing you a song he wrote about the whole business. Hell, they even buried the woman up in the Zapata cemetery on the edge of town. People go up there and look at her grave all the time."

That's what Danny had come for, to see if anybody knew where Luz had been buried. Out of curiosity he asked what had happened to the shooter's body. One of the gringos said the killer had also been buried in the Zapata cemetery, but that someone had stolen the marker and the exact location of the grave had been forgotten.

To Danny, the whereabouts of the shooter's bones wasn't all that important, anyhow. After knowing Clayton Price and listening to him talk about his life and work, Danny had started believing there'd always be shooters, and along the line somewhere he remembered what Sir Thomas Browne once said: "But who knows the fate of his bones or how often he is to be buried." He figured a Clayton Price was still out there in one form or another, shade or otherwise, settling into his bubble and looking down a 9x scope.

Danny told the local constable he was a brother of the woman's first husband and had come to claim her body. The constable didn't believe him. Danny flashed fifty bucks and the constable believed him. The constable even helped dig up Luz's grave and lift the plain pine coffin into the bed of Danny's pickup. Danny drove back to Route 15, headed south, and turned west one more time, passing the village where the ocelot had been caged. The cage was gone from its place under the banana tree.

Outside of Ceylaya he stopped the truck. It took him a long time to drag the coffin up the hill, but he got it done, sweating and panting and resting now and then, and trying to ignore rattling sounds from inside the box. Flies everywhere, driving him half crazy, but he worked through the afternoon, digging a new grave for Luz. He eased her coffin down into the hole and shoveled dirt over it, all the while crying so hard he couldn't see what he was doing most of the time.

Toward sunset he finished and walked back down to the truck. In Escuinapa, he'd had a small marker fashioned out of stone. In Spanish, it read

María de la Luz Santos
1971–1993

Nothing Remains
But Flowers and Sad Songs

He lugged the stone up the hill and set it firmly at the head of the grave. Scouting around in the nearby fields, he picked some red flowers and then laid them on the fresh-shoveled dirt. Danny Pastor stood there for a long time, leaning on the shovel. The image of Luz teaching the shooter to dance that evening in Zapata kept coming back. The yellow dress . . . the flower in her hair . . . his big clumsy steps . . . music playing. And he remembered her humming softly after she'd returned from Clayton Price's room that night. And he remembered hot salsa music and Luz smiling and coming naked across a Puerto Vallarta room toward him with "La Rosa Negra" booming out of the Panasonic.

Darkness had rolled over the Mexican countryside when he passed the ocelot's former place of imprisonment. Danny slowed the truck and looked out across the fields. Nothing there, of course. The cat was probably in a dirty traveling zoo by now or on the back of some rich woman in Paris. What the hell, you do what you can.

When Danny got to Route 15, he leaned forward, resting on the wheel, looking up and down the highway at headlights rolling hard in both directions, diesel trucks and cars and silver green Pacífico buses, long lines of them. After a while he turned left . . . and late . . . much too late and alone . . . toward *el Norte.*

Acknowledgments

Thanks go to my wife, Georgia Ann, who first heard this story in Puerto Vallarta a while back and said it sounded true and worth the telling. She sat through several interviews with various people, helped me piece the story together, and we did a preliminary layout of the book during two evenings we spent in a place called Las Palomas, both of us drinking a little Pacífico along the way and sitting at a particular table where you can put your back against the wall and sweep the room and see who comes in, who's walking along Aldama on your left, and what's happening out on Ordaz.

Thanks to Kathe Goldstein for watching over the Spanish terms, to Mary Ellen Rochester and Gary Thompson for background information on Puerto Vallarta, and to Carol Johnson, Susan Rueschhoff, Gary Goldstein, Linda Kettner, Bill Silag, and Shirley Koslowski, all of whom read various versions of the manuscript and offered helpful advice. And thanks to Sam Cavness, cowboy and veteran of the Vietnam jungles, for his reading of the manuscript. Also, thanks to Audrey Farrell, who worked as my assistant for several years and did her best to keep me organized during the time I was writing this.

And, of course, *muchas gracias* to my friend J. R. Ackley of Marble Rock, Iowa, who twice accompanied me to Mexico as my driver. Even though the U.S. State Department was advising travelers not to use the road to Durango because of heavy bandit activity and we were headed that way, I said "absolutely not" when J.R. wanted to take his .45 automatic pistol with him (though, I must admit, there were several occasions in the backcountry when I wished we'd taken the gun). Shorn of the .45, J.R. nonetheless moved us in safety and good humor along hot, busy roads and through quiet mountains, while I thought about Danny and Luz and a shadowman named Clayton Price, and how all of this must have felt to them during their run for *el Norte*.

The quote dealing with the medicinal properties of beer is J.R.'s. He came up with it at the tail of a hot, dusty day when we had finished a long hike up a remote riverbed and spent time with a man named Don Francisco Quintera, who calls himself the "Keeper of Guadalupe."

Thanks, many thanks, to my friends Willie Royal, violinist, and Lobo, flamenco guitarist, for all the soaring nights of magic in a place called Mamma Mia. I listened to tapes of their music while writing portions of this book (Willie & Lobo, *Gypsy Boogaloo* and *Fandango Nights*, both on Mesa Records). And to all of my friends at the special inn where I have stayed many times in Puerto Vallarta, who have been so kind and helpful. And also to Daniel, who gave us somewhere to rest in the mountains, in a small village near the Durango road, and told us stories of the Mexican outback. And to the old men of the village I have called Zapata here, who lean their chairs against the walls of their village, smoking and resting and talking after a day in the fields.

Certain phrases contained in the fictional account of Clayton Price's dossier, in "Shadowman," were taken directly from James W. Clarke, *American Assassins* (Princeton University Press, 1982).

Finally, I need to mention a curious and haunting circumstance involving background research for this story. While we drove through Mexico on our first scouting trip, tracing the exact route of Luz, Danny, and Clayton Price, J.R. told me about a book describing the life and times of a famous

296

sniper in Vietnam. He couldn't remember the name of the book but said it was fairly obscure and that I would have trouble finding it. After several weeks on the road, we checked out of our small Mexican hotel in Puerto Vallarta to catch our flight home. As I was headed for the taxi, I walked by a counter serving as a book exchange for guests of the hotel. There was only one book on the shelf, well thumbed and hard used, *the* book: *Marine Sniper*. As anyone who's been around will tell you, it gets strange out there.

The employees of THORNDIKE PRESS hope you have enjoyed this Large Print book. All our Large Print books are designed for easy reading — and they're made to last.

Other Thorndike Large Print books are available at your library, through selected bookstores, or directly from us. Suggestions for books you would like to see in Large Print are always welcome.

For more information about current and upcoming titles, please call or mail your name and address to:

THORNDIKE PRESS
PO Box 159
Thorndike, Maine 04986
800/223-6121
207/948-2962